Molly Elliot Seawell

A Strange, Sad Comedy

Molly Elliot Seawell

A Strange, Sad Comedy

ISBN/EAN: 9783744767972

Printed in Europe, USA, Canada, Australia, Japan

Cover: Foto ©Andreas Hilbeck / pixelio.de

More available books at **www.hansebooks.com**

A STRANGE, SAD COMEDY

BY

MOLLY ELLIOT SEAWELL

AUTHOR OF "THE SPRIGHTLY ROMANCE OF MARSAC," "CHILDREN OF
DESTINY," "MAID MARIAN AND OTHER STORIES"
"LITTLE JARVIS," ETC.

NEW YORK
THE CENTURY CO.
1896

A STRANGE, SAD COMEDY

A STRANGE, SAD COMEDY

I

ONE sunny November day, in 1864, Colonel Archibald Corbin sat placidly reading "The Spectator" in the shabby old library at Corbin Hall, in Virginia. The Colonel had a fine, pale old face, clean shaven, except for a bristly, white mustache, and his white hair, which was rather long, was combed back in the fashion of the days when Bulwer's heroes set the style for hairdressing. The Colonel — who was no more a colonel than he was a cheese-box — had an invincible placidity, which could not be disturbed by wars or rumors of wars. He had come into the world in a calm and judicial frame of mind, and meant to go through it and out of it calmly and judicially, in spite of rude shocks and upheavals.

Everything about Colonel Corbin had reached the stage of genteel shabbiness — a shabbiness which is the exclusive mark of gentlemen. His dignified frock-coat was white about the seams with much brushing, and the tall, old-fashioned " stock " which supported his chin was neatly but obviously mended. The furniture in the room was as archaic as the Colonel's coat and stock. A square of rag carpet covered the floor; there had been a Brussels carpet once, but that had long since gone to the hospital at Richmond—and the knob of the Colonel's gold-headed cane had gone into the collection-plate at church some months before. For, as the Colonel said, with a sort of grandiose modesty — " I can give but little, sir, in these disjointed times. But when I do give, I give like a gentleman, sir."

There had been a time, not long before that, when he had been compelled to "realize," as the Virginians euphemistically express it, upon something that could be converted into cash. This was when it became necessary to bring the body of his only son, who had been killed early in the war, back to Corbin Hall — and likewise to bring the dead man's twelve-year-old daughter from the far South, where her mother had quickly followed her father across

the gulf. Even in that sad extremity, the Colonel had never dreamed of "realizing" on the
great piles of silver plate, which would, in those
times, have commanded instant sale. The
Corbins, who were perfectly satisfied to have
their dining-room furnished with some scanty
horsehair sofas and a few rickety chairs and
tables, had a fancy for loading down rude cup-
boards with enough plate for a great establishment, according to a provincial fashion in
Virginia. But instead of this, the Colonel sacri-
ficed a fine threshing-machine and some of his
best stock without a qualm. The Colonel had
borne all this, and much more,—and the
rare, salt tears had worn little furrows in his
cheeks,—but he was still calm, still composed,
under all circumstances.

The sun had just marked twelve o'clock on
the old sun-dial in the garden, when the Colonel, happening to glance up, saw Aunt Tulip,
the dairymaid, streaking past the window,
with her petticoat over her head, followed by
Nancy, the scullion, by little Patsy Jane, who
picked up chips for the kitchen fire, by Tom
Battercake, whose mission in life was indicated
by his name,— the bringing in of battercakes
being an important part of life in Virginia,—

and by Juba, who was just beginning his apprenticeship by carrying relays of the eternal battercakes from the kitchen to the dining-room. And the next moment, Miss Jemima, the Colonel's sister and double, actually danced into the room with her gray curls flying, and gasped, " Brother, the Yankees are coming ! "

" Are they, my dear Jemima?" remarked the Colonel, rising. " Then we must prepare to meet them with all the dignity and composure possible." As the Colonel opened the door, his own man, Dad Davy, nearly ran over him, blurting out the startling news, " Marse, de Yankees is comin' ! " and the same information was screeched at him by every negro, big and little, on the plantation who had known it in time to make a bee-line for the house.

" Disperse to your usual occupations," cried the Colonel, waving his hand majestically. The negroes dispersed, not to their business, but with the African's natural love of a sensation to spread the alarm all over the place. By the time it got to the "quarters," — the houses of the field-hands, farthest away from "de gret house," — it was reported that Dad Davy had told Tom Battercake that he saw Aunt Tulip "runnin' outen de gret house, and the Yankees wuz hol'in er pistol at ole Marse' hade, and

Miss Jemima, she wuz havin' er fit with nobody but little Patsy Jane," etc., etc., etc. What really happened was, the Colonel walked calmly out in the hall, urging Miss Jemima to be composed.

" My dear Jemima, do not become agitated. David, you are an old fool. Thomas Batter-cake, proceed to your usual employment at this time of day, cleaning the knives, or what-ever it is. Would you have these Yankee mis-creants to think us a body of Bedlamites?"

Just then, down the stairs came running pretty little twelve-year-old Letty, his grand-daughter. Letty seized his veined and ner-vous hand in her two pink palms, and expressed a willingness to die on the spot for him.

The Colonel marched solemnly out on the porch, and by that time, what seemed to him an army of blue-coats was dashing across the lawn. A lieutenant swung himself off his horse, and, coming up the steps, demanded the keys of the barn, in a brogue that could be cut with a knife.

" No, sir," said the Colonel, firmly, his gray hair moved slightly by the autumn wind, "you may break open my barn-door, but I decline to surrender the keys."

The lieutenant, at that, struck a match

against the steps, and a little point of flame was seen among the withered tendrils of the Virginia creeper that clung to the wooden pillars of the porch.

"Now, will you give up those keys, you obstinate ould ribil?" asked the lieutenant, fiercely.

"No!" responded the Colonel, quite unmoved. "The term that you apply to me is the one that was borne with honor by the Father of his country. Moreover, from your accent, which I may be permitted to observe, sir, is grotesque to the last degree, I surmise that you yourself may be a rebel to Her Majesty, Queen Victoria, for certainly there is nothing American about you."

At this, a general snicker went around among the enemy, for discipline was not very well observed between officers and men in those days. Then, half a dozen cavalrymen dropped off their horses and made for the well, whence they returned in a twinkling with water to put out the fire that had begun to crackle ominously. The Colonel had not turned a hair, although Miss Jemima behind him and Letty had clung together with a faint cry.

The lieutenant rode off in the direction of the barn, ordering most of the men to follow him. Wagons were then seen coming down the lane, and going toward the barn to cart off the Colonel's corn and wheat. The sympathies of those who were left behind were plainly with the Colonel. Especially was this so with a tall, lanky, grizzled sergeant, who had been the first man to put out the fire.

"I am much obliged to you, my good man," said Colonel Corbin, loftily, "for your efforts in extinguishing the flames started by that person, who appears to be in command."

"You 're welcome," answered the lanky sergeant, with the easy familiarity of the rural New-Englander.

The lieutenant had showed unmistakably the bullying resentment of a peasant brought face to face with a gentleman, but the lanky sergeant indirectly felt some subtile sympathy with a spirit as independent as his own.

"I am glad, brother," said Miss Jemima, "that these men who are left to guard us are plainly Americans. They will be more humane than foreigners."

"Vastly more so," answered the Colonel, calmly watching the loading of his crops upon

the wagons in the distance. "There is, particularly in New England, a sturdy yeomanry,
such as our friend here belongs to," indicating
the sergeant, "which really represents an admirable type of man."

"Gosh," exclaimed the sergeant, in admiration, "it's the durndest, gamest thing I ever
see, you standin' up here as cool as a cucum-
ber, when your property's bein' took. I kin
stand fire; my grandfather, he fought at Lex-
ington, and he did n't flunk nuther, and I ain't
flunked much. But I swan, if you Johnny Rebs
was a-cartin' off my hay and stuff, I'd be a deal
more excited 'n you are. And my old woman
—gosh t' almighty!"

The lanky sergeant seemed completely staggered by the contemplation of the old woman's
probable behavior upon such an occasion.

"There are other things, my friend," answered the Colonel, putting his hands under
his coat-tails and turning his back upon the
barn in the distance, "which are of more consequence, I opine, than hay and corn. That,
I think, the most limited intelligence will
admit."

"That's so," responded the lanky sergeant,
"I kin do a sight better keepin' bees up in

Vermont than down here in Virginny fightin'
the rebs for eighteen dollars a month, but when
Uncle Abe called for seventy-five thousand
men I could n't a-kep' them bees another day,
not if I had been makin' two hundred dollars
a month at it.   When I heard 'bout it, I kem
in, and I said to the old woman : ' I 've got a
call,' and she screeched out, ' A call to git converted, Silas ?'—the old woman 's powerful re-
ligious,—and I says, ' No, Sary—a call to go
and fight for the Flag.'   And when we talked
it over, and remembered about my grandfather,
— he lived to be selectman, — the old woman
says, ' Silas, you are a miser'bul man, and
you 'll git killed in your sins, and no insurance
on your life, and it 'll take all I kin rake and
scrape to bring your body home, but mebbe
it 's your duty to fight for your country.'   And
she said I might come, and here I am, and the
bees is goin' to thunder."

"Unfortunately for me, sir," said the Colonel, with a faint smile, but with unabated politeness.   "However, I wish to say that you
are pursuing your humble but unpleasant duty
in a most gentlemanlike manner.   For, look
you, the term gentleman is comprehensive.   It
includes not only a man who has had the ad-

vantages of birth and station, — advantages
which I may, with all modesty, claim, as enjoying them without any merit of my own, — but
a man like yourself, of honorable, though humble parentage, who possesses a sturdy independence of spirit to which, I may say, my
friend with the violent brogue is a stranger."

The lanky sergeant, who had a dry, Puri-
tanical humor of his own, was immensely
tickled at this, and, at the same time, profoundly respectful of a man who could enter into
disquisitions respecting what constituted a
gentleman while his goods were being confis-
cated under his very nose.

"I tell you what," said he, becoming quite
friendly and confidential with the Colonel,
"there 's a fellow with our command, — an
Englishman, — and he 's got the same name
as yours — Corbin — only he 's got a handle
to it.   He is Sir Archibald Corbin, and I never
see a young man so like an old one as he is
like you.   He just seems to me to be your very
image.   He ain't reg'larly attached nor nothin';
he 's just one of them aide'campers.   He might
be your son.   Hain't you got any son?"

At this, little Miss Letty, who had kept in
the background clinging to Miss Jemima, came

forward, and the Colonel put one arm around her.

"I had a son, — a noble son, — but he laid down his life in defense of his State, and this is his orphan child," said he.

The lanky sergeant took off his cap and made a bow.

"And I 'll be bound," he said, with infinite respect in his awkwardly familiar manner, "that your son was true grit." He stopped and hunted about in his mind for a title to bestow upon the Colonel superior to the one he had, and finally hit upon "Judge," to which title the Colonel was as much entitled as the one he bore.

"Judge, I don't believe you 'd turn a hair if there was a hundred pieces of artillery trained on you. I believe you 'd just go on talkin' in this 'ere highflown way, without kerin' about anything except your dignity. And if your son was like you, he did n't have no skeer in him at all, General." By this time the sergeant had concluded that the old gentleman deserved promotion even from the title of Judge.

The Colonel inclined his head, a slight flush creeping into his wan face.

"You do me honor," he said, "but you do my son only justice."

By this time the wagons had been loaded up and were being driven off. The scared negroes that had flocked about the house from all over the plantation were peering, with ashy faces, around the corners and over the garden fence. The men were ordered to fall in, the lieutenant giving his orders at a considerable distance, and in his involuntary and marked brogue. The lanky sergeant and the few men with him mounted, and then all of them, simultaneously, took off their caps.

"Three cheers for the old game-cock!" cried the lanky sergeant enthusiastically. The cheers were given with a will and with a grin. The Colonel bowed profoundly, smiling all the time.

"This is truly grotesque," he said. "You have just appropriated all of my last year's crops, and now you are assuring me of your personal respect. For the last, I thank you," and so, with cheering and laughter, they rode off, leaving the Colonel with his self-respect unimpaired, but minus several hundred bushels of corn and wheat. The negroes gradually quieted down, and the Colonel and Miss Jemima and little Miss Letty retired to the library. The Colonel took down his family tree, and began gravely to study that perennially entertaining document in order to place the Corbin who was serving as aide-de-camp in the Union army. Miss Jemima, too, was deeply interested, and remarked sagely:

" He is no doubt a great-grandson of Admiral Sir Archibald Corbin, who adhered to the royal cause and was afterward made a baronet by George III."

At that very moment, the Colonel hit upon him.

" That is he, my dear Jemima. General Sir George Corbin, grandson of the admiral and son of Sir Archibald Corbin, second, married to the Honorable Evelyn Guilford-Hope, has one son and heir, Archibald, born May 18, 1842. His father must be dead, and he has but little more than reached his majority. Sister, if he were not in the Federal army, I should be most happy to greet him as a kinsman. But I own to an adamantine prejudice toward strangers who dare to meddle in civil broils."

So had Miss Jemima, of course, who regarded the Colonel's prejudices as direct inspirations from on high.

The very next week after the visitation of the Federal cavalry came a descent upon the part of a squad of Confederate troopers. As the Colonel and Miss Jemima entertained the commanding officers in the library, with the most elaborate courtesy and home-made wine, the shrill quacking and squawking of the ducks and chickens was painfully audible as the hungry troopers chased and captured them. The Colonel and Miss Jemima, though, were perfectly deaf to the clamor made by the poultry as their necks were wrung, and when a cavalryman rode past the window with one of Miss Jemima's pet bronze turkeys hanging from his saddle-bow and gobbling wildly, Miss Jemima only gave a faint sigh, and looked very hard at little Miss Letty, who was about to shriek a protest against such cruelty. Even next morning she made not a single inquiry as to the startling deficit in the poultry yard. And when Aunt Tulip began to grumble something about "dem po' white trash dat cum ter a gent'-mun' house, an' cornfuscate he tu'keys settin' on the nes'," Miss Jemima shut her up promptly.

"Not a word, not a word, Tulip. Confederate officers are welcome to anything at Corbin Hall."

A few nights after that, the Colonel sat in the library looking at the hickory fire that danced up the chimney and shone on the polished floor, and turned little Letty's yellow hair into burnished gold.   Suddenly a terrific knocking resounded at the door.

In those strange times people's hearts sometimes stood still when there was a clamor for entrance; but the Colonel's brave old heart went on beating placidly. Not so Dad Davy's, who, with a negro's propensity to get up an excitement about everything, exclaimed solemnly:

" D'yar dee come to bu'n de house over we all's hades.   I done dream lars night 'bout a ole h'yar cotch hade fo'mos' in er trap, an' dat 's a sho' sign o' trouble and distrus'-fulness."

" David," remarked the Colonel, according to custom, " you are a fool.   Go and open the hall door."

Dad Davy hobbled toward the door and opened it.   It was about dusk on an autumn night, and there was a weird half-light upon the weedy lawn, and the clumps of gnarled acacias, and the overgrown carriage drive of pounded oyster-shells.   Nor was there any light in the large, low-pitched hall, with its hard mahogany sofa, and the walls ornamented with riding-whips and old spurs. A tall and stalwart figure stood before the door, and a voice out of the darkness asked:

" Is this the house of Mr. Archibald Corbin, and is he at home?"

The sound of that voice seemed to paralyze Dad Davy.

" Lord A'mighty," he gasped, " 't is Marse Archy's voice. Look a heah, is you — is you a *ha'nt?* "[1]

" A what?"

But without waiting for an answer Dad Davy scurried off for a moment and returned with a tallow candle in a tall silver candlestick. As he appeared, shading the candle with one dusky hand, and rolling two great eyeballs at the newcomer, he was handed a visiting card. This further mystified him, as he had never seen such an implement in his life before; he gazed with a fixed and frightened gaze at the young man before him, and his skin gradually turned the ashy hue that terror produces in a negro.

" Hi, hi," he spluttered, " you is de spit and

---

[1] A ghost.

image o' my young Marse, that was kilt long
o' dis lars' year.   And you got he voice.   I
kin mos' swar you wuz Marse Archy Corbin,
like he wuz fo' he got married."

"And my name is Archibald Corbin, too,"
said the young man, comprehending the
strange resemblance between himself and the
dead and gone Archy that had so startled the
old negro. He poked his card vigorously into
Dad Davy's hand.

"What I gwine to do with this heah?"
asked Dad Davy, eyeing the card suspiciously.

"Take this card to your master."

"And if he ax me who k'yard 't is, what I
gwi' tell him?"

At this the young man burst out into a
ringing, full-chested laugh.   The negroes
were new to him, and ever amusing, and he
could not but laugh at Dad Davy's simplicity.
That laugh brought the Colonel out into the
hall. He advanced with a low bow, which the
stranger returned, and took the card out of
Dad Davy's hand, meanwhile settling his
spectacles carefully on his nose, and reading
deliberately :

"Sir Archibald Corbin, Fox Court."

The Colonel fixed his eyes upon his guest,

and, like Dad Davy, the resemblance to the other Archibald Corbin overcame him instantly. His lips trembled slightly, and it was a moment or two before he could say, with his usual blandness:

" I see you are Archibald Corbin, and I am your kinsman, also Archibald Corbin."

" Being in your neighborhood," said Sir Archibald, courteously, " I could not forbear doing myself the pleasure of making myself known to the only relatives I have on this side of the water."

There was something winning and graceful about him, and the Colonel was much surprised to find that any man born and bred outside of the State of Virginia should have so fine an address.

" It gives me much gratification," replied Colonel Corbin, in his most imposing barytone, " to acknowledge the relationship existing between the Corbins of Corbin Hall in Virginia and those of Fox Court in England."

In saying this he led the way toward the library, where two more tallow dips in silver candlesticks had been lighted.

When young Corbin came within the circle of the fire's red light — for the tallow dips did

not count — Miss Jemima uttered a faint
scream. This strange sensation that his appearance made in every member of the family
rather vexed the young Englishman, who was
a robust specimen, and with nothing uncanny
about him, except the strange and uncomfortable likeness to a dead man whom he had
never seen or heard of until that moment.

" Pardon me," said the Colonel, after a moment, in a choked voice, "but your resemblance to my only son, who was killed while
gallantly leading his regiment, is something
extraordinary, and you will perhaps understand a father's agitation "— here two scanty
tears rolled down upon his white mustache.
Even little Miss Letty looked at the new
comer with troubled eyes and quivering lips.

Young Corbin, with a hearty and healthy
desire to get upon more comfortable subjects
of discourse, mentioned that, having a taste for
adventure, he had come to America during
the terrible upheaval, and through the influence of friends in power he had obtained a
temporary staff appointment, by which he was
able to see something of actual warfare.

This statement was heard in absolute
silence. Young Corbin received a subtile

impression that his new-found relatives rather disapproved of him, and that the fact that he was a baronet with a big rent-roll, which had hitherto brought him the highest consideration, ranked as nothing with these primitive people. Naturally, this was a stab to the self-love of a young fellow of twenty-two, but with the innate independence of a man born to position and possessions, he refrained from forcing his consequence upon his relatives. The Colonel talked learnedly and eloquently upon the subject of the Corbins and their pedigree, to which Miss Jemima listened complacently. Little Miss Letty, though, seemed to regard the guest as a base intruder, and glowered viciously upon him, while she knitted a large woolen sock.

Supper was presently announced by Dad Davy. There might be a rag carpet on the floor at Corbin Hall, and tallow dips, but there was sure to be enough on the table to feed a regiment. This supper was the most satisfactory thing that young Sir Archy had seen yet among his Virginia relations. There was an "old ham" cured in the smoke from hickory ashes, and deviled turkey after Miss Jemima's own recipe, and it took Tom Batter-

cake, Black Juba, and little Patsy Jane, all together, to bring in supplies of batter-cakes,
to which the invariable formula was: "Take
two, and butter them while they are hot."

The Colonel kept up a steady fusillade,
reinforced by Miss Jemima, of all the family
history, peculiarities, and what not, of the
Corbin family. The Corbins were, to a man,
the best judges of wines in the State of Virginia; they inherited great capacity for whist;
and were remarkable for putting a just esti-
mate upon people, and inflexible in maintaining their opinions. "Of which," said the
Colonel, suavely, "I will give you an example:

"My honored father always believed that it
was the guest's duty, when spending the night
at a house, to make the motion toward retir-
ing for the night. My uncle, John Whiting
Corbin, held the contrary. As both knew
the other's inflexibility they avoided ever
spending the night at each other's houses, although upon the most affectionate and bro-
therly terms. Upon one occasion, however,
my uncle was caught at Corbin Hall by stress
of weather. The evening passed pleasantly,
but toward midnight the rest of the family,
including my sister Jemima and myself, re-

tired, leaving my father and his brother amicably discussing the Virginia resolutions of '98.
As the night wore on both wished to retire,
but my father would not transgress the code
of etiquette he professed, by suggesting bed-
time to his guest, nor would my uncle yield
the point by making the first move.

"When, at daylight the next morning, my
boy Davy came in to make the fire, here, sir,
in this library, I assure you, my father and
his brother were still discussing the resolutions
of '98.   They had been at it all night."

This was one of the Colonel's crack stories,
and Sir Archy laughed at it heartily enough.
But with all this studied hospitality toward
himself, he felt more, every moment, in spite
of the Colonel's sounding periods, that he was
merely tolerated, at best, and as he had never
been snubbed before in his life, the experience
did not please him.   At ten o'clock he rose to
go, saying that he preferred traveling by
night under the circumstances.   The Colonel
invited him to remain longer, with careful
politeness, but when the invitation was declined, no more was visible than civil regret.
Nevertheless, the Colonel went himself to see
that Sir Archy's horse had been properly fed

and rubbed down, and Miss Jemima went to
fetch a glass of the home-made wine, which
nearly choked Sir Archy in the effort to gulp
it down. He was alone for a few moments
with pretty little Letty, who had not for a
moment abandoned her standoffish attitude.

"Will you be glad to see me the next time
I come, little cousin?" he asked, mischievously.

Here was a chance for Letty to annihilate
this brazen new-comer, and she proceeded to
do it by quoting one of the Colonel's most elaborate phrases. She got slightly mixed on the
word "adamantine," but still Letty thought it
sounded very well when she remarked, loftily,
"I have an anti-mundane prejudice toward
foreigners meddling in domestic broils." And
every word was punctuated by a scowl.

Miss Letty fondly imagined that the young
Englishman would be awed and delighted at
this prodigious remark in one so young, but
when Sir Archy burst into one of his rich and
ringing laughs, Letty promptly realized that
he was laughing at her, and could have pulled
his hair with pleasure.

Sir Archy was still laughing and Letty was
still blushing and scowling when their elders
returned. In a little while Sir Archy was

galloping down the sandy lane at Corbin Hall, with the faint lights of the grim old house twinkling far behind him.   It was an odd experience, and not altogether pleasing.   For once, he had met people who knew he was a baronet, and who did not care for it, and who knew he had a great property, and who did not feel the slightest respect for it.   There was something sad, something ludicrous, and something noble and disinterested about those refined, unsophisticated people at Corbin Hall; and when that little sulky, frowning thing grew up, she would be a beauty, Sir Archy decided, as he galloped along the sandy road through the moonlight night.

II

EN summers after this, the old Colonel and Miss Jemima and Miss Letty scraped up money enough to spend a summer in a cheap boarding-house at Newport. Many surprises awaited the Colonel upon his first visit to Newport since "before the war, sir." In the first place, the money they paid for their plain rooms seemed a very imposing sum to them, and they were extremely surprised to find how small it was regarded at Newport.

"Newport, my dear Jemima and Letty, is a more expensive place than the White Sulphur in its palmiest days, when it had a monopoly of the chivalry of the South," announced the Colonel, oracularly.

Letty had innocently expected a great triumph, especially with her wardrobe. She had no less than five white Swiss muslin frocks, all tucked and beruffled within an inch of her life, and she had also a lace parasol, besides one that had belonged to her mother, and several lace flounces and a set of pearls. This outfit, thought Letty, vain and proud, was bound to make a sensation. But it did not. However, no matter what Letty wore, she was in no danger of being put behind the door. First, because she was so very, very pretty, and second, because she was so obviously a thoroughbred, from the sole of her little arched foot, up to the crown of her delicate, proud head. And Letty was so extremely haughty. But she soon found out that Swiss muslin frocks don't count at Newport, and that even a Corbin of Corbin Hall, who lodged in a cheap place, was not an object of flattering attention.

And the more neglected she was, the more toploftical she became. So did the Colonel, and so did Miss Jemima. Walking down Bellevue avenue with the Colonel, Letty would criticize severely the stately carriages, the high-stepping horses and the superbly dressed women and natty men that are characteristic of that swell drive. But when a carriage would pass with a crest on its doors, the Colonel's white teeth showed beneath his mustache in a grim smile.

"One of the Popes," he remarked, with suave sarcasm, "who started in life as a cobbler, took for his papal arms a set of cobblers' tools. But I perceive no indication whatever, in this community of retired tradespeople, that they have not all inherited their wealth since the days of the Saxon Heptarchy."

For a time it seemed as if not one single person at Newport had ever heard of Colonel Archibald Corbin, of Corbin Hall. But one afternoon, as Letty and her grandfather were taking a dignified promenade,—they could not afford to drive at Newport,—they noticed a stylish dogcart approaching, with a hale, manly fellow, neither particularly young nor especially handsome, handling the ribbons. Just as he caught sight of the Colonel he pulled up, and in another moment he had thrown the reins to the statuesque person who sat on the back seat, and was advancing toward the old man, hat in hand.

"This must be Colonel Corbin. I can't be mistaken," he cried, in a cordial, rich voice.

Letty took in at a glance how well set up he was, how fresh and wholesome and manly.

"It *is* Colonel Corbin," replied the Colonel, with stately affability.

"But you don't remember me, I see. Perhaps you recall my father, John Farebrother—wines and liquors. We're not in the business now," he said, smiling, turning to Letty with a sort of natural gracefulness, "but, contrary to custom, we have n't forgotten it."

The Colonel seized Farebrother's hand and sawed it up and down vigorously.

"Certainly, certainly," he said. "Your father supplied the cellars of Corbin Hall for forty years, and the acquaintanceship begun in a business way was continued with very great pleasure on my part, and I frequently enjoyed a noble hospitality at your father's villa here, in the good old days before the war."

"And I hope you will extend the same friendship to my father's son," said Farebrother, still holding his hat in his hand, and looking very hard at Letty, as if to say, "Present me."

"My granddaughter, Miss Corbin," explained the Colonel, and Letty put her slim little hand, country fashion, when she was introduced, into the strong, sunburned one that Farebrother held out to her. Farebrother nodded to the statuesque person in the dogcart, and his nod seemed to convey a whole code of meaning. The dogcart trundled off down the road, and Farebrother walked along by Letty's side, the Colonel on the other. Letty examined this new acquaintance critically, under her dark lashes, anxiously endeavoring to belittle him in her own mind. But having excellent natural sense, in about two minutes and a half she recognized that this man, who mentioned so promptly that his father dealt in wines and liquors, was a gentleman of the very first water. In fact, there is no discounting a gentleman.

Almost every carriage that passed caused Farebrother to raise his hat, and Letty took in, with feminine astuteness, that he was a man of large and fashionable acquaintance. He walked the whole way back to their dingy lodgings with them, and then went in and sat in the musty drawing-room for half an hour. What had Miss Corbin seen at Newport? he asked. Miss Corbin had seen nothing, as she acknowledged with a faint resentment in her voice. This Mr. Farebrother pronounced a shame, a scandal, and a disgrace. She must immediately see everything. His sisters would call immediately; he would see to that. His

mother never went out. He hoped to see
Miss Corbin at a breakfast or something or
other his sisters were planning. They had
got hold of an Englishman with a handle to
his name, and although the girls pretended
that the Britisher was only an incident at the
breakfast, that was all a subterfuge. But
Miss Corbin should judge for herself, and
then, after thanking the Colonel warmly for his
invitation to call again, Farebrother took his
leave.

The very next afternoon, an immaculate
victoria drove up to the Corbins' door, and
two immaculately stylish girls got out. Miss
Jemima and the Colonel were not at home, so
Letty received the visitors alone in the grim
lodging-house parlor. They got on famously,
much of the sweetness and true breeding of
the brother being evident in the sisters. They
were very English in their voices and pronun-
ciation and use of phrases, but in some way it
did not sound affected, and they were genuinely kind and girlishly cordial. And it was
plain that "our brother" was regarded with
extreme veneration. Would Miss Corbin
come to a breakfast they were giving next
Saturday? Miss Corbin accepted so delight-

edly, that the Farebrother girls, who were not accustomed to Southern enthusiasm over trifles, were a little startled.

Scarcely had the young ladies driven off when up came Mr. Farebrother. Letty, at this, their second meeting, received him as if he had been a long lost brother. He, however, who knew something about the genus to which Letty belonged, grinned with keen appreciation of her rapturous greeting, and was not the least overpowered by it. He hung on in the most unfashionable manner until the Colonel arrived, who was highly pleased to meet his young friend, as he called Farebrother, who had a distinct bald spot on the top of his head, and the ruddy flush of six-and-thirty in his face. Farebrother desired the Colonel's permission to put him up at the Club, and offered him various other civilities, all of which the Colonel received with an inconceivably funny air of conferring a favor instead of accepting one.

Newport assumed an altogether different air to the Corbins after the Farebrother raid. But Letty's anticipations of the breakfast were dashed with a little secret anxiety of which she was heartily ashamed. What should she wear?

She had never been to a fashionable breakfast before in her life. She hesitated between her one elaborate gown, and one of her fresh muslins, but with intuitive taste she reflected that a white frock was always safe, and so concluded to wear one, in which she looked like a tall white lily.

The day of the breakfast arrived; the noonday sun shone with a tempered radiance upon the velvety turf, the great clumps of blue and pink hydrangeas, and the flower borders of rich and varied color, on the shaven lawns. It was a delicious August forenoon, and the warm and scented air had a clear and charming freshness. The shaded piazzas of the Farebrother cottage, with masses of greenery banked about them, made a beautiful background for the dainty girls and well-groomed men who alighted from the perfect equipages that rolled up every minute. Presently a " hack " in the last stage of decrepitude passed through the open and ivy-grown gateway, and as it drew up upon the graveled circle, Letty Corbin, in her white dress and a large white hat, rose from the seat. Farebrother was at her side in an instant, helping her to descend. Usually, Letty's face was of a clear and creamy paleness, but now it was flushed with a wild-rose blush. It had suddenly dawned upon her that the ramshackly rig, which was quite as good as anything she was accustomed to in Virginia, did not look very well amid the smart carriages that came before and after her. However, it in no wise destroyed her self-possession, as it would have done that of some of the girls who descended from the smart carriages. And there was Farebrother with his kind voice and smile, waiting to meet her at the steps, and pouring barefaced compliments in her ear, which last Miss Letty relished highly.

The two girls received her cordially, and introduced her to one or two persons. But they could not devote their whole time to her, and in a little while Letty drifted into the cool, shaded, luxurious drawing-room, and found that she was left very much to herself. The men and girls around her chatted glibly among themselves, but they seemed oblivious of the fact that there was a stranger present, to whom attention would have been grateful. Two very elegant looking girls talked directly across her, and were presently joined by a man who quite ignored her even by a glance, and although she sat between him and the girls, he

kept his eyes fixed on them. Letty thought
it was very bad manners.

"At Corbin Hall," she thought bitterly, "a
stranger would have been overwhelmed with
kind attentions"; but apparently at Newport
a stranger had no rights that a cottager was
bound to respect.

"The fact is, Miss Cornwell," said the man,
in the studied, low voice of the "smart set,"
"I 've been nearly run off my legs this week
by Sir Archy Corbin. He 's the greatest fellow for doing things I ever saw in my life.
And he positively gives a man no rest at all.
We 've always been good friends, but I shall
have to 'cut him' if this thing keeps up."

The lie in this statement was not in the
least obvious to Letty, but was perfectly so to
the young women, who knew there was not
the remotest chance of Sir Archy Corbin being
cut by any of their set. The name, though, at
once struck Letty, and her mobile face showed
that she was interested in the subject.

"Will he be at the meet on Thursday, Mr.
Woodruff?" asked the girl, suddenly dropping
her waving fan and indolent manner, and showing great animation. At this, Woodruff answered with a slightly embarrassed smile:

"Well — er — no, I hardly think so. You know, in England, this is n't the hunting season —"

"Oh, no," struck in Miss Cornwell, perfectly at home in English customs, "their hunting season is just in time to break up the New York season."

Letty's face, which was very expressive, had unconsciously assumed a look of shocked surprise. Hunting a fox in August! For Letty knew nothing of the pursuit of the fierce and cunning aniseseed bag. Her lips almost framed the words, "How dreadful!"

Woodruff, without glancing at her, but taking in swiftly the speaking look of disgusted astonishment, framed with his lips something that sounded like "Society for the Prevention of Cruelty to Animals."

A blush poured hotly into Letty's face. The rudeness of talking about her before her face angered her intensely, but did not for a moment disconcert her. There was a little pause. Miss Cornwell looked straight before her with an air of amused apprehension. Then Letty spoke in a clear, soft voice:

"You are mistaken," she said, looking Woodruff calmly in the face. "I do not be-

long to that society.   I do not altogether believe in professional philanthropy.   I was, it
is true, shocked at the idea of fox-hunting in
August, because, although I have been accustomed to seeing hunting in a sportsmanlike
manner all my life, the fox was given a chance
for his life."

It was now Woodruff's turn to blush, which
he did furiously.   He was not really a rude
man, but his whole social training had been in
the line of trying to imitate people of another
type than himself, and consequently his per-
ceptions were not acute.   The imitative process is a blunting one.   But he did not desire
to give anybody pain, and the idea of a social
blunder was simply harrowing to him.

" Pray excuse me," he said, and looked a
picture of awkward misery, and Miss Cornwell
actually seemed to enjoy his predicament.

Letty had instantly risen as soon as she had
spoken, but by the time she had taken a step
forward there was a little movement in front
of her, and the next moment she saw the same
Sir Archibald Corbin she had seen ten years
ago, standing in front of her, holding out his
hand and saying: " May I ask if this is not
my cousin, Miss Corbin, of Corbin Hall? You

were a little girl when I saw you last, but I
cannot be mistaken."

" Yes, I am Letty Corbin," answered Letty,
giving him her hand, impulsively; she would
have welcomed her deadliest enemy at that
moment, in order to create a diversion.

But the effect of this meeting and greeting
upon Woodruff and Miss Cornwell, and the
people surrounding them, was magnetic.   If
Letty had announced, "I am the sole and only
representative of the noble house of Plan-
tagenet," or Howard, or Montmorenci, their
surprise could not have been greater.

Sir Archy spoke to them with that cool
British civility which is not altogether pleasing.   Woodruff had time to feel a ridiculous
chagrin at the footing which his alleged friend
put him on, and Letty was quite feline enough
to let him see it.   She fixed two pretty, malicious eyes on him, and smiled wickedly when
instead of making up to Sir Archy, he very
prudently turned toward Miss Cornwell, who
likewise seemed secretly amused.

But Sir Archy's manner toward Letty was
cordiality itself.   He asked after the Colonel.

" And such a royal snubbing as I got from
him that time so long ago," he said, fer-

vently. "I hope he has no intention of re-
peating it."

"I can't say," replied Letty, slyly, and ex-
amining her cousin with much approval. He
had the delicious, fresh, manly beauty of the
Briton, and he had quite lost that uncanny
likeness to a dead man which had been so
remarkable ten years ago. He had, however,
the British simplicity which takes all of an
American girl's subtilities in perfect candor
and good faith. He and Letty got along
wonderfully together. In fact, Letty's fluency
and affability was such that she could have
got on with an ogre. But presently Farebrother came up and carried her off, under Sir
Archy's very nose, toward the dining-room.
As Letty walked across the beautiful hall into
the dining-room beyond, some new sense of
luxury seemed to awaken in her. She was
familiar enough with certain elegancies of life,
— at that very moment she had her great-
grandmother's string of pearls around her
milky-white throat, — and Corbin Hall contained a store of heirlooms for which the average Newport cottager would have bartered
all his modern bric-à-brac. But this nicety
of detail in comfort was perfectly new and de-

lightful to her, and she confided so much to
Farebrother.

"You see," she complained, confidentially,
"down in Virginia we spend all we have on
the luxuries of life, and then we have to do
without the necessaries."

"I see," answered Farebrother, "but then
you 've been acknowledged as a cousin by an
English baronet. Think of that, and it will
sustain you, and make you patient under
your trials more than all the consolation of
religion."

"I 'll try to," answered Letty, demurely.

"And he is a first-rate fellow, too," continued Farebrother, who could be magnani-
mous. "I made up to him at the club before
I knew who he was—"

"Oh, nonsense. You knew he was a baronet."

"I 'll swear I did n't. Presently, though, it
leaked out that he was what the newspapers
call a titled person. We were talking about
some red wine that a villain of a steward was
trying to palm off on us, and Sir Archy gave
his opinion, which was simply rubbish. I told
him so in parliamentary language, and when
he wanted to argue the point, I gently re-

minded him that my father and my grandfather had been in the wine-importing line, and I had been born and bred to the wine business."

By this time Farebrother's light-blue expressive eyes were dancing, and Letty fully took in the joke.

" The descendants of the dealers in tobacco, drugs, and hardware, who were sitting around, were naturally much pained at my admission, but Sir Archy was n't, and actually gave in to my opinion. He stuck to me so close — now, Miss Corbin, I swear I am not lying — that I could n't shake him off, and he walked home with me. Of course I had to ask him in, and then the girls came out; they could n't have been kept away from him unless they had been tied, and he has pervaded the house more or less ever since. That is how it is that the noble house of Corbin is to-day accepting the hospitality of the humble house of Farebrother."

"Very kind of us, I 'm sure," said Letty, gravely, "but I 'd feel more important if I had more clothes. You can't imagine how fine my wardrobe seemed down in Virginia, and here I feel as if I had n't a rag to my back."

"A rag to your back, indeed," said Farebrother, with bold admiration. "Those white
muslin things you wear are the prettiest gowns
I ever saw at Newport."

Letty smiled rapturously. The breakfast
was delightful to two persons, Letty Corbin
and Tom Farebrother. After it was over they
went out on the lawn, and watched the long,
soft swell of the summer sea breaking at their
feet, and the gay hydrangeas nodding their
pretty heads gravely in the sunshine. And in
a moment or two Sir Archy came up and
joined them. Farebrother held his ground
stoutly; he always held it stoutly and pleasantly as well, and the three had such a jolly
time that the correct young ladies who used
their broad a's so carefully, and the correct
young gentlemen in London-made morning
clothes, stared at such evident enjoyment. But
it was a respectful stare, and even Letty's
ramshackly carriage was regarded with toler-
ation when it rattled up. Sir Archy, however,
asked permission to drive her back in his
dog-cart, which Letty at once agreed to,
much to Tom Farebrother's frankly expressed
disgust.

"There you go," he growled in her ear.

"Just like the rest; the fellow has a handle to his name and that 's enough."

"Why did n't you offer to drive me home yourself?" answered Letty, with equally frank coquetry, bending her eyes upon him with a challenge in their hazel depths.

"By George, why did n't I?" was Farebrother's whispered reply, as he handed her over to Sir Archy.

Miss Corbin's exit was much more imposing than her arrival, as she drove off, sitting up straight and slim, in Sir Archy's dog-cart.

"Do you know," said he, as they spun along the freshly watered drive in the soft August afternoon, "that you are the first American I have seen yet? All of the young ladies that I see here are tolerably fair copies of the young ladies I meet in London drawing-rooms; but you are really what I fancied an American girl to be."

"Thank you," answered Letty, dubiously. "But I daresay I am rather better behaved than you expected to find me."

"Not at all," answered Sir Archy, with energy.

This was a good beginning for an acquaintance, and when Letty got home she could not

quite decide which she liked the better, Tom
Farebrother or this sturdy, sensible English
cousin.

It is scarcely necessary to say that Letty's
fortune was made as far as the Newport season
went. Her opinions of people and things at
Newport underwent a sudden change when
she began to be treated with great attention.
She triumphantly confided to both Farebrother
and Sir Archy that she did not mean to let
the Colonel start for Virginia until he had
spent all his money, and she had worn out all
her clothes, and would be obliged to go home
to be washed and mended. Meanwhile she
flirted infamously and impartially with both,
after a manner indigenous to the region south
of Mason and Dixon's line.

III

THE period so frankly mentioned by Letty, when the party from Corbin Hall would get to the end of their financial tether, arrived with surprising promptness. But something still more surprising happened. The Colonel quite unexpectedly had dumped upon him the vast and imposing sum of two thousand dollars. This astonishing fact was communicated to Farebrother one sunny day when he and Letty were watching a game of tennis at the Casino.

"Do you know," said she, turning two sparkling eyes on him from under her large white hat, and tilting her parasol back gaily, "we are not going away, after all."

"Thank the Lord," answered Farebrother, with fervent irreverence.

He had found out that he could talk any amount of sentiment to Letty with impunity. In fact, she rather demanded excessive senti-

ment, of which she nevertheless believed not
one word. Farebrother, who had seen something of Southern girls, very quickly and ac-
curately guessed that it was the sort of thing
Letty had been used to. But he was amused
and charmed to find, that along with the most
inveterate and arrant coquetry, she combined
a modesty that amounted to prudery, and a
reserve of manner in certain respects which
kept him at an inexorable distance. He could
whisper soft nonsense in Letty's ear all day
long, and she would listen with an artless enjoyment that was inexpressibly diverting to
Farebrother. But when he once attempted to
touch her hand in putting on her wrap, Letty
turned on him with an angry stare that disconcerted him utterly. It was not the surprise of an ignorant girl, but the thorough
resentment of an offended woman. Farebrother
took care not to transgress in that way again.

Letty fully expected him to express rapturous delight at her announcement, and was
not disappointed. "It 's very strange," she
continued, twirling her parasol and leaning
forward in her chair; "grandpapa's father lent
some money a long time ago,—I think the
Corbins got some money by hook or by crook

in 1814,—and they lent it all out, and ever since then they have been borrowing, as far as I can make out. Well, some of it was on a mortgage that was foreclosed the other day, so grandpapa says, and he got two thousand dollars."

Letty held off to watch the effect of this stunning statement. Two thousand dollars was a great deal of money to her. Farebrother, arrant hypocrite that he was, had learned the important lesson of promptly adopting Letty's view of everything, and did it so thoroughly that sometimes he overdid it.

"Why, that 's a pot of money," he said gravely. "It 's quite staggering to contemplate."

Letty was not deficient in shrewdness, and she knew by that time that the standard of values in Virginia and at Newport varied. So she looked at him very hard, and said, sternly:

"I hope you are not telling me a story."

"Of course not. But really," here Farebrother became quite serious, "it depends a good deal on how it comes. Last year, for example, I only made three thousand dollars.

You see I 've got enough to live upon without
work, and that 's a fearful drawback to people
giving me work. I 'm an architect, and I love
my trade. But I can't convince people that
I 'm not a *dilettante*. I am ashamed to eat
the bread of idleness, and yet — here 's a question that comes up. Has any man a right,
who does not need to work, to enter into close
competition with those who do need it ? "

Farebrother was very much in earnest by
that time. He saw that these nineteenth-cen-
tury problems had never presented themselves
to Letty's simple experience. But they were
of vast moment to him. Letty fixed her large,
clear gaze upon him very much as if he were
a new sort of animal she was studying.

" I thought here, where you are all so rich,
you cared for nothing except how to enjoy
yourselves."

" Did you ? Then you made a huge mistake. Why, I know of men literally wallow-
ing in money who work for the pure love of
work. I could work for love of work, too, but
I tell you, when I see a poor fellow, with a
wife and family to support, slaving over plans
and specifications, and then I feel that my
competition is making that man's chances con-

siderably less, it takes the heart out of my work. Now, if you 'll excuse me, I 'll say that I could make three thousand dollars several times over if I went at it for a living — because like all men who work from love, not from necessity, I am inclined to believe in my own capacity and to have a friendly opinion of my own performances. You may disparage everything about me, and although it may lacerate my feelings, I will forgive you. But just say one word against me as an architect, and everything is over between us."

" I sha'n't say anything against you or your architecture either," replied Letty, bringing the battery of her eyes and smile to bear on him with shameless cajolery.

But just then their attention was attracted by a group approaching them over the velvet turf. Sir Archibald Corbin was in the lead, escorting two tall, handsome, blonde young women. They were evidently sisters and evidently English. They had smooth, abundant light hair, knotted low under their turban hats, and their complexions were deliciously fresh. Although the day was warm, and Letty found her sheer white frock none too cool, and every other woman in sight had on a thin light gown,

these two handsome English women wore
dark, tight-fitting tweed frocks, and spotless
linen collars. Behind them walked two men,
one a thoroughly English-looking young fellow, while the last of the party so completely
fixed Letty's attention as soon as she put her
eyes on him, that she quite forgot everybody
else.

He was an old man, small, slight, and scrupulously well dressed. His hair was perfectly
white, and his face was bloodless. His clothes
were a pale gray, his hat was a paler gray,
and he was in effect a symphony in gray.
Even the rose at his buttonhole was white.
But from his pallid face gleamed a pair of the
blackest and most fascinating eyes Letty had
ever beheld. It was as if they had gained in
fire and intensity as his blood and his life
grew more sluggish. And however frail he
might look, his eyes were full of vitality. He
walked along, leaning upon the arm of the
young man and speaking but little. The party
stopped a little way off to watch a game of tennis, while Sir Archy made straight for Letty.

"May I introduce my friends to you?" he
asked, in a low voice. "Mrs. Chessingham,
and her sister, Miss Maywood, Chessingham

and Mr. Romaine. Chess is one of the best
and cleverest fellows going, and of good family, although he is a medical man, and he is
traveling with Mr. Romaine — a rich old hypochondriac, I imagine."

As soon as he mentioned Mr. Romaine a
flood of light burst upon Letty. "Is n't he a
Virginian? — an American, I mean? And
did n't grandpapa know him hundreds of
years ago?" she asked, eagerly.

"I have heard he was born in Virginia, as
poor Chessingham knows to his cost," answered Sir Archy, laughing quietly. "After
having gone all over Europe, Asia, and Africa,
the old hunks at last made up his mind that he
would come back to America. Chess was very
well pleased, particularly as Mrs. Chessingham
and Miss Maywood were invited to come as his
guests. But old Romaine swears he means to
take the whole party back to Virginia to his
old place there that he has n't seen for forty
years, and naturally they 'll find it dull."

Sir Archy possessed in perfection that ap-
palling English frankness which puts to shame
the characteristic American caution. But Sir
Archy's mistake was Farebrother's opportunity.

"Deuced odd mistake, finding Virginia dull," remarked that arch hypocrite, at which Letty rewarded him with a brilliant smile.

Sir Archy had got his permission by that time, and he went across the grass to his friends and brought them up.

The two English women looked at Letty with calmly inquisitive eyes full of frank admiration. Letty, with a side-look and an air of extreme modesty, took them from the top of their dainty heads to the soles of their ugly shoes at one single swift glance. Then Mr. Chessingham was presented, and last, Mr. Romaine. Mr. Romaine gave the impression of looking through people when he looked at them and nailing them to the wall with his glance. And Letty was no exception to the rule. He fixed his black eyes on her, and said in a peculiarly soft, smooth voice: "Your name, my dear young lady, is extremely familiar to me. Archibald Corbin and his brothers were known to me well in my youth at Shrewsbury plantation."

"Mr. Archibald Corbin is my grandfather, and he has spoken often of you," replied Letty, gazing with all her eyes.

This then was Mr. Romaine, the eccentric,

the gifted Mr. Romaine, of whose career vague
rumors had reached the quiet Virginia country
neighborhood which he had left so long ago.
Far back in the dark ages, about 1835, when
Colonel Corbin had made a memorable trip in
a sailing-vessel to Europe, Mr. Romaine had
been an attaché of the American legation in
London; he had resigned that appointment,
but he seemed to have taken a disgust to his
native country, and had never returned to it.
And Letty had a dim impression of having
heard that Miss Jemima in her youth had had
a slight weakness for the handsome Romaine.
But it was so far in the distant past as to be
quite shadowy.   There was a superstition
afloat that Mr. Romaine had made an enormous fortune in some way, and his conduct
about Shrewsbury certainly indicated it.   The
place had been farmed on shares for a generation back, and the profits paid the taxes,
and no more.   But the house, which was a
fine old mansion, had never been suffered to
fall into decay, and was kept in a state of
repair little short of marvelous in Virginia.
Nobody was permitted to live in it, and at
intervals of ten years the report would be
started that Mr. Romaine intended returning

to Shrewsbury. But nothing of the sort had been said for a long time now, and meanwhile Mr. Romaine was on the American side, and nobody in his native county had heard a word of it.

"And Miss Jemima Corbin," said Mr. Romaine, a faint smile wrinkling the fine lines about his mouth. "When I knew her she was a very pretty young lady; there have been a great many pretty young ladies in the Corbin family," he added, with old-fashioned gallantry.

"Aunt Jemima is still Miss Corbin," answered Letty, also smiling. "She never could find a man so good as my grandfather, 'brother Archibald,' as she calls him, and so she would not have any at all."

"May I ask if your grandfather is here with you? and is he enjoying good health?"

"Yes, he is now in the Casino — I don't know exactly where, but he will soon come for me."

This reawakening of his early life was not without its effect on Mr. Romaine, nor was it a wholly pleasant one. For time and Mr. Romaine were mortal enemies. His face flushed slightly, and he sat down on a garden

chair by Letty, and the next moment Colonel
Corbin was seen advancing upon them. The
Colonel wore gaiters of an ancient pattern;
they were some he had before the war. His
new frock-coat was tightly buttoned over his
tall, spare figure, and on his head was a broad
palmetto hat. In an instant the two old men
recognized each other and grasped hands.
They had been boy friends, and in spite of
the awful stretch of time which had separated
them, and the total lack of communication between them, each turned back with emotion to
their early associations together.

Then the Colonel was presented to the two
ladies, who seemed to think that there was a
vast and unnecessary amount of introducing
going on, and the younger people formed a
group to themselves. Letty and Miss Maywood fell to talking, and Letty asked the
inevitable question:

"How do you like America?"

"Quite well," answered Miss Maywood, in
her rich, clear English voice. "Of course the
climate is hard on us; these heats are almost
insufferable. But it is very interesting and
picturesque, and all that sort of thing. Mr.
Romaine tells us the autumn in Virginia,

where he is to take us to his old place, is beautiful."

" Mr. Romaine's place and our place, Corbin Hall, are not far apart," said Letty, and at once Miss Maywood felt a new interest in her.

" Pray tell me about it," she said.   " Is it a hunting country ? "

" For men," answered Letty. " But I never knew of women following the hounds. We sometimes go out on horseback to see the hunt, but we don't really follow the hounds."

" But there is good hunting, I fancy," cried Miss Maywood with animation. " Mr. Romaine has promised me that, and I like a good stiff country, such as he tells me it is.   I have hunted for four seasons in Yorkshire, but now that Gladys has married in London, she has invited me to be with her for six months in the year, and although I hate London, I love Gladys, and it 's a great saving, too.   But it puts a stop to my hunting."

Letty noticed that not only did Miss Maywood use Mr. Romaine's name very often, but she glanced at him continually. He sat quite close to the Colonel, listening with a half smile to Colonel Corbin's sounding periods, describing the effects of the war and the present status of things in Virginia. His extraordinarily expressive black eyes supplied comment without words.

"I am very glad you are coming to the county," said Letty, after a moment, "and I hope you 'll like Newport, too. At first I did n't like it, but afterward, I met the Farebrothers" — she spoke in a low voice, and indicated Farebrother with a glance — "and they have been very kind to me, and I have had a very good time. We intended to go home next week. Newport 's a very expensive place," she added, with a frank little smile. "But now, we — that is, my grandfather and my aunt and myself — intend staying a little longer."

"Everything in America is expensive," cried Miss Maywood, with energy. "I can't imagine how Mr. Romaine can pay our bills; they are so enormous. Reginald — Mr. Chessingham — is his doctor, you know, and Mr. Romaine won't let Reggie leave him, and Reggie would n't leave Gladys, and Gladys would n't leave me, and so, here we are. It is the one good thing about Reggie's profession. I hate doctors, don't you?"

"Why?" asked Letty, in surprise.

"Because," said Miss Maywood, positively,
"it's so unpleasant to have people saying,
'What a pity—there is that sweet, pretty
Gladys Maywood married to a medical man'—
he is n't even a doctor—and Gladys cannot go
to Court, you know, and it has really made
a great difference in her position in London.
Papa was an army man, and we were presented when we came out; but society has
come to an end as far as poor Gladys is concerned. And although Reggie is a dear fellow, and I love him, I do wish he was n't
associated with plasters and pills and that sort
of thing."

All this was thoroughly puzzling to Letty,
but she had realized since she came to Newport that there was a great, big, wide world,
with which she was totally unfamiliar, outside
of Corbin Hall and its neighborhood. She
knew she was a stranger to the thoughts and
feelings of the people who lived in this outer
world. She glanced at "Reggie"—he had a
strong, sensible face, and she could imagine
that Mr. Romaine might well find help in him.

"Is Mr. Romaine very, very ill?" she asked.

"I don't know," replied Miss Maywood,

smiling. " He 's a very interesting man, rich, and has an excellent position in England. He does n't do a great deal, but he always has strength enough to travel. I think, occasionally, perhaps, he is only hipped, but it would not do to say generally. Sometimes he talks about dying, and sometimes he talks about getting married."

"Who would marry him, though?" asked Letty, innocently.

"Who *would n't* marry him?" replied Miss Maywood, calmly. "There was a French woman a few years ago—" She stopped suddenly, remembering that she knew very little about this French woman, a widow of good family but small means. There had been a subdued hurricane of talk, and she remembered hearing that at the time wagers had been made as to whether the French woman would score or not. But Mr. Romaine had apparently outwitted Madame de Fonblanque,— that was her name,— and since the Chessinghams had been with him, nothing had been seen or heard of the French widow. So Miss Maywood merely said in her gentle, even way, "I grant you, he is n't young, and his health is not good, but his manners and his

money are above reproach, and so is his position." Miss Maywood mentally added to this
last qualification — " for an American."

" Marrying for manners, money, and position
does n't strike me as quite a nice thing to do,"
said Letty, stoutly.

Miss Maywood simply glanced at her, but
the look said as plainly as words, " What a
fool to suppose anybody would believe you."

But what she actually said was, with a little
laugh, " That 's very nice to say, but marriage
without those things is out of the question, and
the possession of them marks the difference
between a possible man and an impossible
man."

This short discussion had brought the two
young women to a mutual contempt of one
another, although each was too well bred to
show it. Just then there was a slight diversion
in the group, and Letty gravitated toward Sir
Archy. It was then his turn instead of Farebrother's to receive assurances of Miss Corbin's distinguished consideration.

" Where have you been all the morning ? "
she asked, with her sweetest wheedling. " I 've
been looking out for you a whole hour."

Farebrother was then engaged with Mrs.

Chessingham and Miss Maywood, and did not
hear this colossal fib, which would not have
ranked as a fib at all in Letty's birthplace.
But Miss Maywood heard it with a thrill of
disgust. Not so Sir Archy. He had found
out by that time that the typical American girl
— *not* the sham English one, which sometimes
is evolved from an American seedling — is
prone to say flattering things to men, which
cannot always be taken at their face value.
Nevertheless, he liked the process, and showed
his white teeth in a pleasant smile.

"And," continued Letty, with determined
cajolery, "you really must not treat me with
the utter neglect you 've shown me for the
last ten days."

"Neglect, by Jove," said Sir Archy, laughing. "It seems to me that the neglect you
complain of keeps me on the go from morning
till night. When I am not doing errands for
you I am reading up on subjects that I have
never thought essential to a polite education
before, but which you seem to think anybody
but a Patagonian would know."

Nothing escaped Miss Maywood's ears.
"The brazen thing," she thought indignantly
to herself. "Pretending that she would n't

marry for money and position and now simply
throwing herself at Sir Archy's head."

Letty, however, was altogether unconscious
of this, and went on with happy indifference.

" I found your knowledge of the American
Constitution perfectly rudimentary, and of
course I could not condescend to talk to any
man ignorant of the first principles of our government, and you ought to go down on your
knees and thank me for putting you in the
way of enlightenment."

Every word Letty uttered startled Miss
Maywood more and more. It was bad enough
to see Sir Archy swallowing the huge lumps
of flattery that Miss America so calmly ad-
ministered, but to see him take mildly a hec-
toring and overbearing attack upon the one
subject — public affairs — on which a man is
supposed to be most superior to woman was
simply paralyzing. Miss Maywood turned,
fully expecting to see Sir Archy walk off in
high dudgeon. Instead of that he was laughing at Letty, his fine, ruddy face showing a
boyish dimple as he smiled.

Then there was a move toward the Casino.
Somebody had proposed luncheon. Colonel
Corbin and Mr. Romaine got up from their

seats and joined the younger people. The Colonel, with a flourish of his hand, remarked to Mrs. Chessingham, " You have witnessed, madam, the meeting of two old men who have not seen each other in more than forty years. A very gratifying meeting, madam ; for although all retrospection has its pain, it has also its pleasure."

This allusion to himself as an old man evidently did not enrapture Mr. Romaine. His eyes contracted and he scowled unmistakably, while the Colonel, with a bland smile, fondly imagined that he had said the very thing calculated to please. Farebrother took the lead, and the party was soon seated at a round table, close to a window that looked out upon the gay lawns and tennis grounds. Then Letty had a chance to study Mr. and Mrs. Chessingham and Mr. Romaine a little more closely.

Mr. Chessingham was unmistakably prepossessing. He had in abundance the vitality, the steadiness of nerve, the quiet reserve strength most lacking in Mr. Romaine. There was a healthy personal magnetism about the young doctor which accounted for Mr. Romaine's willingness to saddle himself with all of Chessingham's impedimenta. Mrs. Chess-

ingham, although as like Miss Maywood as
two peas, yet had something much more soft
and winning about her. She was, it is true,
strictly conventional, and had the typical
English woman's respect for rank and money
and matrimony, but marriage had plainly done
much for her. She might grieve that "Reggie"
could not go to Court, but she did full justice
to Reggie as a man and a doctor.

Miss Maywood sat next Mr. Romaine, and
agreed scrupulously with everything he said.
This peculiarity of hers seemed to inspire the
old gentleman with the determination to make
a spectacle of her, and he advanced some of
the most grotesque and alarming fallacies
imaginable, to which Miss Maywood gave a
facile assent.

"It is my belief," he said, quite gravely, at
last, in consequence of an allusion to the
Franco-Prussian war, "that had the Communists succeeded in keeping possession of Paris
a month longer, we should have seen the
German army trooping out of France, and
glad to get away at any price. Had the
Communists' intelligent use of petroleum been
made available against the Prussians, who
knows what the result might have been? I

have always thought the few disorders they committed very much exaggerated, and their final overthrow a misfortune for France."

"Great heavens!" exclaimed Colonel Corbin, falling back in his chair; but finding nothing else to say, he poured out a glass of Apollinaris and gulped it down in portentous silence.

"No doubt you are right," said Miss Maywood, turning her fresh, handsome face on Mr. Romaine. "One never can get at the truth of these things. The Communists were beaten, and so they were wrong."

There was a slight pause, during which Sir Archy and Farebrother exchanged sympathetic grins; they saw how the land lay, and then Letty spoke up calmly.

"I can't agree with Mr. Romaine," she said in her clear voice. "I think the Communists were the most frightful wretches that ever drew breath. To think of their murdering that brave old archbishop."

"Political necessity, my dear young lady," murmured Mr. Romaine. "M. Darboy brought his fate on himself."

"However," retorted Letty with a gay smile, "it is just possible that you may be guying us. The fact is, Mr. Romaine, your eyes are too expressive, and when you uttered those terrific sentiments, I saw that you were simply setting a trap for us, as deep as a well and as wide as a church door. But we won't walk in it to please you."

Miss Maywood colored quickly. It never had occurred to her literal mind before that Mr. Romaine did not mean every word he said, and if she had thought to the contrary, she would not have dared to say it. She fully expected an outbreak of the temper which Mr. Romaine was known to possess, but instead, as with Sir Archy, Letty's daring onslaught produced only a smile. Mr. Romaine was well pleased at the notion that he was not too old to be chaffed.

"You are much too acute," he said, with a sort of silent laughter.

"Just what I have always told Miss Corbin," remarked Farebrother, energetically. "If you will join me, perhaps we can organize a society for the suppression of clever women, and then we sha'n't be at their mercy as we now are."

"And don't forget a clause guaranteeing that they shall be deprived of all opportunities of a higher education," suggested Sir Archy,

5

who had learned by that time to forward any joke on hand.

"That would be unnecessary," said Mr. Romaine. "The higher education does them no harm at all, and gives them much innocent pride and pleasure."

As the luncheon progressed Miss Letty became more and more in doubt whether she liked Mr. Romaine or not. She regarded him as being somewhere in the neighborhood of ninety-five, and wished to feel the respect for him she ought to feel for all decent graybeards. But Mr. Romaine was as fully determined not to be thought old as Letty was determined to think that he was old. He was certainly unlike any old man that she had ever met; not that there was anything in the least ridiculous about him,— he was much too astute to affect juvenility,— but there was an alertness in his wonderful black eyes and a keenness in his soft speech that was far removed from old age. And he was easily master of everybody at the table, excepting Farebrother and Letty. With feminine intuition Letty felt Mr. Romaine's power, and knew that had Mr. Chessingham been the old man and Mr. Romaine the young doctor, Mr. Romaine would still have been in the ascendant. The Colonel, with well meant but cruel persistence, tried to get Mr. Romaine into a reminiscent mood, but in vain. Mr. Romaine utterly ignored the "forty years ago, my dear Romaine," with which Colonel Corbin began many stories that never came to a climax, and he positively declined to discuss anything that had happened more than twenty years before. In fact this peculiarity was so marked that Letty strongly suspected that the old gentleman's memory had been rigidly sawed off at a certain period, as a surgeon cuts off a leg at the knee-joint.

The Chessinghams evidently enjoyed themselves, and the utmost cordiality prevailed, except between the two girls, who eyed each other very much as the gladiators might have done when in the arena for the fray. Still they were perfectly polite, and showed a truly feminine capacity for pretty hypocrisy. Nevertheless, when the luncheon was over and the party separated, Miss Maywood and Miss Corbin parted with cordial sentiments of mutual disesteem. Scarcely were the two sisters alone at the hotel, before Miss Maywood burst forth with, " Well, Gladys, I suppose you see what the typical American girl is! Did you ever hear anything equal to Miss Corbin's language to Mr. Romaine and Sir Archy? Actually rating them! And then the next moment plying them with the most outrageous flattery."

"And yet, Ethel, she seemed to please them," answered Mrs. Chessingham, doubtfully. "But I was a little scandalized, I admit."

"A little scandalized! Now, I do assure you, leaving out of account altogether any personal grievance about these two particular men, I never heard a girl talk so to men in all my life."

Ethel told the truth this time and no mistake.

"Nor did I," said Mrs. Chessingham. "But perhaps she's not a fair type."

"Did n't Sir Archy tell us she was the most typical American that he has yet seen? And does n't Mr. Romaine know all about her family? And really," continued Miss Maywood, getting off her high horse, and looking genuinely puzzled, "I scarcely know whether it would be right for me to make a companion of such a girl; you know her home is in the same county as Mr. Romaine's place, quite near, I fancy — and we have been so carefully brought up by dear mama, and so often warned against associating with reckless girls, that I am not quite sure that we ought to know her when we go to Virginia."

Here Mrs. Chessingham's confidence in Reggie came to her help.

"Now don't say that, Ethel dear. Reggie thinks her a charming girl, and you saw for yourself nobody seemed to take her seriously except ourselves, so the best thing for you to do is to go on quietly and be guided by circumstances."

"But the way she made eyes!" said Miss Maywood, disgustedly. "It's perfectly plain she means to marry either Mr. Romaine or Sir Archy — she advertises the fact so plainly that she 'll probably overshoot the mark. At all events, I shall be on my guard, and unless I am much mistaken, you will find that we can't afford to know her."

Meanwhile Letty, in the little sitting-room of their lodgings, was haranguing Colonel Corbin and Miss Jemima upon Miss Maywood's iniquities.

"The most brazen piece, Aunt Jemima, actually saying that any girl would marry that

old pachyderm, Mr. Romaine! I would n't
marry him if he was padded an inch thick
with thousand-dollar bills! But she as good
as said *she* would—and the way he poked fun
at her! She agrees with everything he says,
and she is making such a dead set at him that
she can't see the old gentleman's game. I am
perfectly disgusted with her."

At the first mention of Mr. Romaine's name,
a faint color came into Miss Jemima's gentle,
withered face.

"Don't speak of him that way, Letty dear,"
she said. "He was a charming man once.
But, perhaps, my love, it would be more prudent for you to avoid Miss Maywood. Nothing is more dangerous to young girls than
association with others who lack modesty and
refinement, as you represent this young lady."

"I 'll think over it," answered the prudent
Letty, who at that moment remembered that
they were all going to the country, which is
dull for young people at best, and a new
neighbor is a distinct godsend not to be trifled
with. But in her heart she had grave doubts
of Miss Maywood's propriety.

IV

IT might be supposed that the modest sum of money, which seemed like a million to Colonel Corbin, would have been used in paying off some of the incumbrances on Corbin Hall, or at least in refitting some part of it. A few hundreds might have been spent very judiciously in stopping up the chinks and crannies of the house, in replacing the worn carpets and having the rickety old furniture mended. But far were such thoughts from the Colonel, Miss Jemima, or Letty. Money was a rare and unfamiliar commodity to all of them, and when they got any of it they wisely spent it in pleasuring. New carpets and sound furniture were not in the least essential to these simple folk, and would have altogether spoiled the harmony of the comfortable shabbiness that prevailed at Corbin Hall. So the Colonel proposed to stop a month or two in New York in order to disburden themselves of this inconvenient amount of cash.   Farebrother found out involuntarily, as indeed everybody else did, the state of affairs, and he took positive delight in the simplicity and primitiveness of these sweet and excellent people, to whom the majesty of the dollar was so utterly unknown.

So admirably had Mr. Romaine got on with the Corbin party, in spite of the Colonel's continual efforts to remind him of the time when they were boys together, that he announced his intention, one night, upon a visit to the little sitting-room appropriated to the Chessinghams, of going to New York the same time the Corbins did, and staying at the same old-fashioned but aristocratic hotel.   The two young women were sitting under the droplight, each with the inevitable piece of fancy work in her hand that is so necessary to the complete existence of an English woman. Mrs. Chessingham glanced at Ethel, whose fine, white skin grew a little pale.

Mr. Romaine sat watching her with something like a malicious smile upon his delicate, highbred old face.   He did not often bestow his company upon his suite, as Letty wickedly called his party.   He traveled in extravagant

luxury, and what with his own room, his sitting-room and his valet's room, and the apart-
ments furnished the Chessinghams and Miss
Maywood, it really did seem a marvel sometimes, as Ethel Maywood said, how anybody
could pay such bills. But he did pay them,
promptly and ungrudgingly. Nobody — not
Chessingham himself — knew how Mr. Romaine's money came or how much he had.
Nor did Mr. Romaine's relatives, of whom he
had large tribes and clans in Virginia, know
any more on this interesting subject. They
would all have liked to know, not only where
it came from, but where it was going to. Not
the slightest hint, however, had been got from
Mr. Romaine during his forty years' sojourn
on the other side. Nor did his unlooked-for
return to his native land incline him any more
to confidences about his finances. There was
a cheque-book always at hand, and Mr. Romaine paid his score with a lofty indifference
to detail that was delightful to women's souls,
particularly to Mrs. Chessingham and Miss
Maywood. Both of them were scrupulously
honest women, and not disposed in the slightest degree to impose upon him. But if he
found out by accident that they had walked

when they might have driven, or had paid for the carriage themselves, or had in any way paid a bill that might have been charged to him, he always chided them gently, and declared that if it happened again all would be over between Chessingham and himself.   This charming peculiarity had caused Ethel to say very often to her sister :

"Although one would much rather marry an Englishman than an American, I don't believe any Englishman alive would be so indulgent to a woman as Mr. Romaine would be.   I have never known any married woman made so free of her husband's money as we are with Mr. Romaine's, and if he does offer himself, I am sure he will make most unheard-of settlements."

But when Mr. Romaine, sitting back in a dark velvet chair which showed off his face, clear cut as a cameo, with his superb black eyes shining full of meaning, spoke of the New York trip, Ethel began to think that there was no longer any hope of that offer. She remained silent, but Mrs. Chessingham, with a pitying glance at her sister, said resignedly, "It will be very pleasant, no doubt. The glimpse we had of New York when we

landed was scarcely enough for so large a
place."

"It is quite a large place," answered Mr.
Romaine, gravely.   "How large should you
take it to be?" he asked Miss Maywood.

"About two or three hundred thousand,"
replied Ethel, dubiously.

"There are four million people within a
radius of ten miles of New York's City Hall.
Good night," said Mr. Romaine, with much
suavity, rising and going.

When he was out of the door Mrs. Chessingham spoke up promptly: "What a story!
I don't believe a word of it."

"Of course it isn't true," complained Ethel,
"but that is the worst of Americans—you
never can tell when they are joking and when
they aren't. As for Miss Corbin, I simply can't
understand her at all. However, this move of
Mr. Romaine's settles one thing. Miss Corbin will be Mrs. Romaine, mark my words."

"Reggie says that there is positively nothing in it; that Mr. Romaine likes her, and is
amused by her. She *is* amusing."

"Yes, I know she is," replied Ethel, ruefully, with something like tears in her voice at
the admission.

"And he says that she would n't marry Mr. Romaine to save his life — and that he has heard her laugh at the idea."

"That only shows, Gladys dear, how blind Reggie is, like the rest of his sex. Of course Miss Corbin protests that she does n't want Mr. Romaine. She did the equivalent to it the very first talk we ever had together, that day at the Casino. But I did n't believe her, and what shocked me was her want of candor. The notion of a girl who does n't want money and position is entirely too great a strain on my credulity. I suppose she 'll say next that she does n't want to be Lady Corbin and live at Fox Court. I think it 's much better to be truthful about things."

"So do I, dear. But my own belief is that she really likes Mr. Farebrother best of all."

"Nonsense," cried Ethel, sharply. "Mr. Farebrother could n't begin to give her Sir Archy's position or Mr. Romaine's money. He 's an architect, with about enough to live on after his father's fortune is cut up into six or seven parts. Not that I pretend to despise Mr. Farebrother; I am truthful in all things, and I think he 's a very presentable, pleasant man, and would be a good match. But to suppose that any girl in her senses would take him in preference to Mr. Romaine or Sir Archibald Corbin is too wildly grotesque for anything. I 'll follow Mr. Romaine's example and say good-night." And off she went.

Sir Archy had begun to find Newport pleasanter day by day. He had wearied in the beginning of the adulation paid to his title and his money, and it soon came to be understood that he was not in the market, so to speak. He found the Farebrother girls pleasant and amiable, and showed them some attention. As he showed none whatever to any other of the cottage girls, nor did he go to any except to the Farebrothers' villa, the family were credited with having laid a deep scheme to monopolize him. The real state of the case was too simple to be understood by artificial people.

Then he had an agreeable sense of familiarity with Mrs. Chessingham and Miss Maywood. They were really well bred and well educated English gentlewomen. Ethel's aloneness had perhaps developed rather too sharply her aspirations toward an establishment of her own, but that is a not uncommon thing among women, and the terrible English frankness brings it to the front without any disguises whatever. Sir Archy, though, knew how to take care of himself among his own countrywomen, as Englishmen do. But he was like clay in the hands of the potter where his American cousin, as he persisted in calling Letty Corbin, was concerned.

Whether Letty was extravagantly fond of him or utterly detested him he could not for the life of him discern. He did discover unmistakably, though, that she was a very charming girl. Her frankness, so different from Ethel Maywood's frankness, was perfectly bewitching. She acknowledged with the utmost candor her fondness for admiration,—her willingness to swallow not only the bait of flattery, but the hook, bob, sinker, and all,—and calmly related the details of her various forms of coquetry. Thus she possessed the charm of both art and simplicity, but, as the case is with her genus, when she fancied she was artful she was very simple, and when she meant to be very simple she was extremely artful.

But she was a delightful and never ending puzzle to Sir Archy. He was manly, clever, and modest, but deep down in his heart was

fixed that ineradicable masculine delusion that
he was, after all, a very desirable fellow for
any girl; and his money and his title had
always been treated as such outward and visible signs of an inward and spiritual grace,
that he would have been more or less than
human if he had not been sanguine of success
if ever he really put his mind to winning any
girl. But Letty was a conundrum to him of
the sort that it is said drove old Homer to
suicide because he could not solve it.

Farebrother, however, understood Letty
and Sir Archy and the Romaine party perfectly, and the little comedy played before his
eyes had a profound interest for him. When
he heard of Mr. Romaine's decision to go to
New York and stay at the same hotel with
the Corbins, he chuckled and shrewdly suspected that Mr. Romaine had in mind more
Miss Maywood's discomfiture than Miss Corbin's satisfaction. He chuckled more than
ever when, on the evening he went to see
the Corbins off on the boat, he found the Romaine party likewise established on deck with
Mr. Romaine's valet and Mrs. Chessingham's
maid superintending the transfer of a van-load
of trunks to the steamer.

They were all sitting together on the upper deck when Farebrother appeared. He carried three bouquets exactly alike, which he handed respectively to Mrs. Chessingham, Miss Maywood, and Letty. Miss Maywood colored beautifully under the thin gray veil drawn over her handsome, aquiline features. Mrs. Chessingham smiled prettily, but Letty's face was a study. A thundercloud would have been more amiable. Farebrother, however, was not in the least disconcerted, but went over to her and smiled at her in a very exasperating manner.

"So kind of you to give us all bouquets alike," began Letty, scornfully.

Meanwhile, in order to keep her chagrin from being obvious to Ethel and Mrs. Chessingham, who would by no means have understood her particularity about attentions, she was cuddling the bouquet as if it were a real treasure.

"I suppose your feeble intelligence was not equal to inventing three separate bouquets for one occasion," she continued, frowning at the offender.

"Yes, it was," answered Farebrother, stoutly. "I knew though that it would thor-

oughly exasperate you, so I did it on purpose."

At this candid defiance Letty's scowl dissolved into a smile.

"I like your childlike innocence," she remarked, "and the way you avow your dis-
honest motives. And I like a man who is a
match for me. I was going to give the
wretched nosegay to the stewardess, but now
I 'll keep it as a souvenir of your delightful
impertinence."

"Thank you," responded Farebrother politely. There was still half an hour before the
boat started, and all three of the young women felt a degree of secret anxiety as to
whether Sir Archy Corbin would be on hand
to bid them good-by. He had spoken vaguely
of seeing them again, and had accepted Colonel Corbin's elaborate invitation to make a
visit at Corbin Hall, but whether he would
depart far enough from his British caution in
dealing with marriageable young women to
see them off on the boat, was highly uncer-
tain.

Miss Maywood, being an eminently reasonable girl, did not fix her hopes too high, and
thought that to be Lady Corbin was too good

6

to be true. Yet it was undeniable that he
seemed to like her, and in this extraordinary
country, where, according to her ideas, there
was a scandalous laxity regarding the value
of attentions, Sir Archy might fall into the
prevailing ways. So she kept her weather
eye open, in spite of the presence of Mr. Romaine, who sat a little distance off slyly watching the bouquet episode and Farebrother.

Letty considered Mr. Romaine merely in
the light of an interesting fossil, but she felt
a characteristic desire to monopolize Farebrother. Besides, at the bottom of her heart
was a genuine admiration for him, and she
felt a sentimental tenderness at the parting
which she fully expected him to share. But
Farebrother was irritatingly unresponsive. He
divided his attentions among the three women
with what was to Letty the most infuriating
impartiality. Nor did he show the downcast
spirits which she fully expected, and altogether his behavior was inexplicable and unsatisfactory.

Letty, however, determined, as the severest
punishment she could inflict, to be very de-
bonair with him, and when at last he seated
himself in the camp chair next hers, she be-

gan upon a flippant subject which she thought
would let Farebrother see that the parting
was as little to her as to him.

"When I get to New York I shall have
some money of my own to spend, and I have
been wondering what I shall do with it," she
said, gravely.

"I am glad to see you appreciate your responsibilities," answered Farebrother.

"Now I know you are making fun of me,"
said Letty, calmly. "But I don't mind. In
the first place, I would like to buy two stained
glass windows for the church which you mis-
erable Yankees wrecked during the war. Have
you any idea of the price of stained glass
windows?"

"I think they run from fifteen dollars up to
twenty or thirty thousand."

"I should n't get a thirty thousand dollar
one, at all events. Then I must have a complete new riding outfit for myself. This comes
of going to Newport. Before that I thought
my riding-skirt, saddle, and bridle quite good
enough, but now I yearn for a tailor made
habit and all the etceteras. How much do
you think that will cost? However, it's not
worth while to ask you, for you would n't be

likely to know. And if you knew, you would n't
tell me the truth."

"Again — thanks."

"And of course I want some clothes —
swell gowns like those I saw at Newport.
And my mother's watch is past repairing any
more, and my piano is on its last legs, and I
promised to bring dear Mrs. Cary, our next
neighbor, an easy-chair for a present, and of
course I shall have to carry Dad Davy and
all the other servants something nice, and I
must make a little gift to Aunt Jemima, and,
and — I 'm afraid my money won't hold out."

"Don't give up," said Farebrother, encour-
agingly. "Leave out the swell gowns, and
the watch, and the piano, and the riding habit,
and I daresay you 'll have enough left for the
rest."

"What do you take me for? To get
nothing for myself? Please understand I am
not so foolish as I look. But, perhaps, after
all, I won't buy any of those things, and I
will lay it all out in a pair of pearl bracelets
to match my mother's necklace, and trust to
luck to get another windfall at some time during my sojourn in this vale of tears."

But Farebrother, who professed to be deeply

interested in this scheme for squandering a fortune, would not let the subject drop. He drew Miss Maywood into the conversation, and although the two girls cordially disliked each other, they were too ladylike to show it, and they had in mind the prospect of spending some months in a lonely country neighborhood, when each might find the other a resource.

"I should think, dear," said the literal Ethel, in her sweet, slow English voice, "that it would be impossible to buy half the things you are thinking of out of that much money, and everything is so ruinously dear in New York, I understand."

"Oh," answered Letty, airily, "it's not the impossibility of the thing that puzzles me; it is the making up of my mind as to which one of the impossibilities I shall finally conclude to achieve."

Miss Maywood thought this a very flippant way of talking, but all American girls were distressingly flippant, except the sham English ones that she met at Newport, who were distressingly serious. And then in a moment or two more a genuine sensation occurred. Sir Archy appeared, red but triumphant, fol-

lowed by his man, and both of them loaded
down with gun-cases, hat-boxes, fishing-reels,
packing-cases, mackintoshes, sticks, umbrellas,
traveling-rugs and pillows, guide-books and
all the vast impedimenta with which an Englishman prepares for a twelve hours' trip as
if he were going to the antarctic circle.

Everybody was surprised to see him, and
to see him in that guise. Mrs. Chessingham
opened her eyes, the ever ready blood flew
into Ethel's fair face, while Letty uttered an
exclamation of surprise.

"You here!" she cried.

"Yes," sighed Sir Archy, beginning to pitch
down his sticks, umbrellas and mackintoshes,
while he heaped a whole cartload of other
things upon the patient valet. "I made up
my mind at the last moment that it would be
deucedly dull without all of you, and here I
am."

Mr. Romaine, who had been sitting at a
little distance, now advanced, his eyes gleaming with a Mephistophelian amusement. In
traveling costume, his make-up was no less
complete than in full evening dress. His perfectly fitting ulster was buttoned closely around
his slight figure; his usual gray hat was re-

placed by a correct traveling-cap; his dog-skin gloves fitted without a wrinkle.   He took in at once the sensation Sir Archy's unex-pected appearance would create in the femi-nine contingent of the party, and he wanted to be on hand to enjoy it.

"We are very pleased to have your com-pany, Sir Archy," he said, blandly, "and still more so if you intend patronizing the same hotel that we shall in New York."

"Thank you," answered Sir Archy, heartily. "I had intended to do so, having been recom-mended by Colonel Corbin."

Just then the Colonel appeared.

"Why, my dear fellow," he cried, in his rich, cordial voice.   "This is truly gratifying.   I thought when I bade you farewell this morn-ing it was for a considerable period, until you paid us that promised visit at Corbin Hall," for the Colonel had become completely recon-ciled to Sir Archy, and had generously over-looked his experiences during the war.

"Yes," said Sir Archy, cheerfully, "I was afraid I'd be a horrid bore, following you all up this way, but I felt so dismal after I had told you good-by—swore so hard at Tomp-kins, and made a brute of myself generally—

that at last I concluded I 'd better pull up stakes and quit."

"Nothing could have been more judicious, my young kinsman," responded the Colonel, "and these ladies, I am sure, are the magnets that have drawn you to us."

"Are you quite sure of that, Corbin?" asked Mr. Romaine, with a foxy smile. "Sometimes a cow does not like to be chased by a haystack."

Sir Archy, still busy with his traps, did not take this in. Ethel Maywood did not contradict it at all. She never took issue with Mr. Romaine, but Letty flushed angrily. She concluded then that Mr. Romaine was very old and very disagreeable.

Farebrother was still lingering, although the first whistle had already blown. It was about nine o'clock on a lovely September evening. The moon had risen, and a pale, opaline glow still lingered on sea and sky, bathing the harbor and the white walled fort and a fleet of yachts in its magic light. The scene and the hour melted Letty. She had been very happy at Newport. Usually, the first taste a provincial gets of the great world beyond is bitter in the mouth, but her experiences had

been rather happy, and of all the men she met,
Farebrother, whose father had made his money
in wines and liquors, and who had conscientious scruples against making money, had
impressed her the most. With the easy confidence born of youthful vanity, and the simplicity of a provincial girl, Letty fancied that
Farebrother would turn up at Corbin Hall
within a month, unable to keep away from her
longer. But at the actual moment of saying
good-by, some lines she had once heard came
back to her—"A chord is snapped asunder
at every parting"—some faint doubt, whether,
after all, he cared enough about her to seek
her out, crossed her mind. Farebrother caught
her eyes fixed on him with a new light in them.
He had begun then to make his good-bys.
Ethel Maywood only felt that general regret
at parting with him that she always felt at
seeing the last of an eligible man—but the
presence of Mr. Romaine and Sir Archy Corbin was more than enough to console her.
All the others, though, were genuinely sorry
—he was so bright, so full of good fellowship,
such a capital fellow all around.

The Colonel wrung his hand for five minutes. He gave Farebrother seven separate

invitations to visit them at Corbin Hall, each
more pressing than the last; he sent his regards to everything at the Farebrother cottage, including the butler. "A very worthy
man, although in an humble station in life,
and particularly attentive to me whenever I
availed myself of your noble hospitality, so
that I did not feel the want of my own serving
man, David, who is equally worthy, although
a great fool."

Miss Jemima pressed Farebrother's hand
warmly, and promised to send him a gallon
of a particular kind of peach cordial which she
knew was very superior to the trashy imported
cordial he had been reduced to drinking.

Letty said nothing, but when Farebrother
came to say good-by to her, she made a deft
movement that took them off a little to themselves, where a word might be said in private
without the others hearing it.

"Good-by," she said, in a voice with a real
thrill in it, such as Farebrother had never
heard before.

He had heard her in earnest about books,
politics, religion, and numerous other subjects,
but seriousness in her tone with men, and especially with men who admired her, was some-

thing new. He held her slim gloved hand in his, and he felt the light pressure of her fingers as she said quickly, in a low voice:

" I sha'n't forget your goodness to me. I hope we shall meet again."

" I hope so too," answered Farebrother, laughing.

The extreme cheeriness of his tone grated upon Letty. She tried to withdraw her hand, but Farebrother held on to it stoutly. A change, too, came over him. His bright, strong face grew tender, and he looked at Letty with a glance so piercing that it forced her to meet his gaze and then forced her to drop her eyes.

" We shall meet again, and soon, if I can compass it; and meanwhile, will you promise not to forget me ?"

A hubbub of talk had been around them. The tramp of the last belated ones hurrying across the gang-plank, and the screaming of the whistle made a commotion that drowned their voices except for each other.

" I promise," said Letty, her heart beginning to beat and her cheeks to flush.

She was very emotional and she was conscious that her eyes were filling with tears and her throat was beginning to throb, and she wanted Farebrother to go before she betrayed herself.

"Good-by, and God bless you," he said, with one last pressure of the hand.

By that time the gang-plank was being hauled in. Farebrother swung himself over the rail to the deck below, ran along the steamer's gangway, and just as the blue water showed between the great hull and the dock, he cleared it at a bound and stood on the pier waving his hat. The gigantic steamer moved majestically out, while handkerchiefs fluttered from her decks and from the dock. It was now almost dark, but as they steamed quickly out into the moonlit bay, Letty fancied she could still distinguish Farebrother's athletic figure in the shadowy darkness that quickly descended upon the shore.

V

NEXT morning, after the usual tussle and struggle for their luggage, in which the whole party, including Mr. Romaine's valet, Sir Archy's man and Miss Maywood's and Mrs. Chessingham's maid took part, they were all driven up to the old-fashioned "before the war" hotel where they had all engaged quarters.

Those for Mr. Romaine and his party were of course the finest in the house, on the drawing-room floor, and the best corner rooms. Sir Archy cared very little where he was put, except that his rooms must be large and have a bath, at which he never ceased to grumble, because there were not shower baths, Turkish baths, Russian baths, and every other arrangement provided for all varieties of bathing.

Colonel Corbin, having in hand what he considered a magnificent sum of money, less a considerable hole in it made by prolonging his stay at Newport, and a present to Letty and a like sum to Miss Jemima, established himself *en prince*. He had a bed-room and sitting-room for himself, besides the bed-rooms and sitting-room for Miss Jemima and Letty. He insisted upon having their meals served in private, but at this Letty flatly rebelled. Go to the public dining-room she would, to see and be seen. The Colonel was no match for Letty when she really put forth her prowess—for liberty or death was that young woman's motto — and in an hour or two after their arrival at the hotel, he very obediently followed her down to the great red-carpeted room, where all the lazy people in the hotel were taking a ten o'clock breakfast.

Letty looked uncommonly charming in her simple, well-fitting gown of dark blue, and masculine eyes were pretty generally turned on her as she entered. But the Colonel attracted still more attention. As he stalked in the great open doorway the head waiter, as imposing as only a black head waiter can be, suddenly exclaimed:

"Hi! Good Lord A'mighty! Ef dis heah ain' Marse Colonel!"

The Colonel recognized his friend in an instant, and extended his hand cordially.

"Why, bless my soul! If it is n't Black Peter, that used to be Tom Lightfoot's body servant! How do you do? how do you do?"

By that time they were sawing the air with mutual delight.

"An' ter think I done live ter see Marse Colonel agin! An' how is all de folks? How ole missis, and Miss Sally Lightfoot, and little Marse Torm?"

"Admirably, admirably well," cried the Colonel, beginning to give all the particulars of ole missis, Miss Sally, little Marse Torm, etc., in his big baritone. The people all turned toward the Colonel and his long-lost friend, and everybody smiled. Letty, not at all confused, stood by her grandfather's side and put her hand into Black Peter's paw.

Peter was extremely elegant, after an antique pattern, not unlike the Colonel's own, and proud to be recognized as a friend by "de fust quality."

He escorted Colonel Corbin and Letty to the most prominent table in the room, called up half a dozen waiters to take their orders, and succeeded in making everybody in the great room see and hear what was going on. He was at last obliged to tear himself away, and the Colonel, while waiting for breakfast, suddenly remembering that he must go to the office to inquire after the health of the room-clerk, who was also an old acquaintance, he left Letty alone for a moment, while he stalked out, magnificently.

Letty had picked up the newspaper and was deep in an editorial on the tariff, when she realized that some one was approaching, and the next moment Farebrother drew a chair up to hers.

For a moment she was too astonished to speak, and simply stared at him, upon which Farebrother began laughing.

"W—where did you come from?" she cried, breathlessly.

"From Newport," answered Farebrother, still laughing at Letty's face.

"And how did you come?"

"By train. Do you suppose when I saw Sir Archy turn up, to come down here, that I meant to be left in the lurch? So I made up my mind in a jiffy, threw a few things in my bag, and made the ten o'clock train; lovely night going down, was n't it?".

"Yes," answered Letty, who was instantly armed with the whole panoply of coquetry, "lovely. I sat out on deck two hours with Sir Archy."

"That was a pretty good stretch for a fellow. There are very few girls who can hold a man's attention that long, and it's rather a dangerous thing to try," said Farebrother, with calm assurance.

"We had a very interesting time," answered Letty, stiffly.

"Oh, yes, I know how an Englishman talks to a girl by moonlight. Tells her about sheep farming, or how he hooked a salmon in the Highlands, or killed a pig in India."

"Our conversation *was* a little on that order," replied Letty, weakly. "But it is a relief to meet with a man who can withstand the influences of the moon and talk sense."

"I never could," said Farebrother, and then he asked for Miss Jemima and the rest of the party. Letty explained that Mr. Romaine and the Chessinghams preferred their meals in their rooms, and the Colonel proposed the same thing to her, but she objected, first, because she liked the liveliness of the public dining-room, and secondly, because it cost

7

more, and she did n't believe in spending money
to make one's self lonely and uncomfortable,
which could generally be done for nothing.

Presently the Colonel reappeared, and was
delighted to see Farebrother, whose arrival
did not surprise him in the least. Farebrother,
who was astute, immediately made a series of
engagements with the Colonel and Miss Jemima and Letty for a drive in Central Park,
a visit to the opera, and various other festivi-
ties, strictly limited to a party of four, from
which he intended Sir Archy should be con-
spicuously left out.

When breakfast was over, and Letty had
gone to prepare for the drive, she met Sir
Archy as she was coming down the stairs,
putting on her gloves.

"Are you going out?" he asked. "I had
my breakfast in my room, and took a spin
around the park before nine o'clock."

"I am going to the park now. Mr. Farebrother takes us. He came down last night,
on the late train."

Sir Archy looked rather black at this. Of
course Farebrother's arrival could mean but
one thing—he had Letty's encouragement to
come. Letty, however, was anxious to dis-

claim all responsibility for his presence in New York. This only puzzled Sir Archy the more. He was not up in the subtility of American flirtations, and regarded Letty's way of playing off as a grave infraction of the moral code. Something of this he hinted to her. At this Letty's gay laughter pealed out.

"Why, don't you suppose that American men know how to take care of themselves?" she cried.

"They ought to — they have opportunities enough to learn," answered Sir Archy, grimly.

But then Letty heard the Colonel's voice, and tripped down the steps, leaving Sir Archy moodily chewing his mustache, and wondering at the depravity of American girls.

The day was bright and beautiful, and there was an autumn crispness in the blue air. Letty leaned back in her own corner of the big easy landau, shading her pretty, thoughtful face with her red parasol. She had on a little black gown, and a large black hat, which suited well her dainty type. Farebrother thought so, sitting opposite her, and watching the look of calm delight in her eyes as they drove along the leafy roads, and stopped in the bosky dells of the park.

There were not many people out—the
"carriage people" had not yet returned to
town, and there was a charming air of peace
and quiet over the scene. The leaves were
beginning to turn, and the caretakers were
busy gathering up piles of those that had
dropped. Occasionally the carriage stopped
in the shade, and the voices of the little party
fell in unison with the faint rustling of the
leaves and the sylvan stillness. Sometimes
they could almost forget that they were near
the throbbing heart of a mighty city.

At one part of the drive, in the very lone-
liest spot they had yet seen, Farebrother proposed to Letty to get out and take a little
stroll. Letty agreed very promptly, and the
Colonel and Miss Jemima concluded they
would stay where they were. So Letty and
her friend strolled away down to the banks of
a little stream, where the dry leaves of the
young trees rustled to the whispering of the
wind. It was high noon then, but so retired
was this spot that the glare was utterly shut
out. Whenever Letty found herself alone
with Farebrother she felt a very acute sympathy between them. She felt this now, more
than usual. Farebrother did not make love
to her in the least with seriousness. Indeed,

he had never done so, and his most suggestive compliments were paid when they were laughing and joking most familiarly. When they were alone, his tone was one of tender friendship and respect, which was very captivating to Letty. She was used to the overflowing sentiment of Southern men, and the calm and sane admiration of a man like Farebrother pleased her with its novelty, and flattered her by its respect.

They stood there a long time, Letty idly throwing pebbles into the stream. They said but little, and that in the low tone to which the voice naturally drops in the woods, and presently, a silence that was full of sweet companionship fell between them. They might have stayed there all day, so charming was it, had not Letty suddenly remembered herself.

"Oh, we must be going," she said.

"Yes," answered Farebrother, with a little sigh, "we must be going."

When they caught sight of the carriage, the Colonel was just about getting out in order to go in search of them. Letty's face grew scarlet, and she was unusually silent on their way home and wished she had not stayed so long alone with Farebrother.

Farebrother had arranged to take the Colonel and Letty to the theater that evening; Miss Jemima had declined. Letty spent the afternoon in her room, resting. At dinner she came out radiant in a white gown, a charming white hat, with white fan and gloves. This, she fondly imagined, was the correct wear for the theater, in orchestra seats. Farebrother had got those seats with a wary design. If he had taken a box, Sir Archy might have found out where they were going, and it is possible to pay visits in a box, and Farebrother determined to have Letty free from the claims of any other man except the Colonel on that one evening. He saw in a moment that Letty had got altogether the wrong ideas about costume, but she looked so fresh and fair that, with masculine indifference to conventionality, he was glad she had put on her white gown.

When dinner was over, and they were waiting in the reception-room for their carriage, the Chessinghams, Ethel Maywood and Mr. Romaine appeared, also bound for the theater, and for the same play that Farebrother had selected. It was the first appearance of a celebrated artist in a play new in this country, and Farebrother had given more attention to the artist than the piece. It was the first

meeting of the whole party since they had
parted on the boat that morning. Mr. Romaine, when he found that they were all
bound for the same performance, grinned
suggestively, and said to Farebrother:

"May I ask if you have ever seen this
piece?"

"No," answered Farebrother, "but I fancy
it's very good. It's an adaptation from the
the French, no doubt made over to suit American audiences, which are the most prudish in
the world."

Mr. Romaine indulged in one of his peculiar
silent laughs. "It is thoroughly French," he
remarked, slyly.

This made Farebrother genuinely uncomfortable. He knew that not only Letty knew
little of the theater, but that she was super-
sensitive as to questions of propriety, and that
this outrageous coquette would not stand one
equivocal word. And the Colonel was as
prudish as she. Farebrother would have
hailed with delight then anything that would
have broken up his party, and wished that he
had suggested the Eden Musée.

Nothing escaped Mr. Romaine's brilliant
black eyes. He took in at once Letty's white

costume, and with malice aforethought, whispered to Miss Maywood:

"Pardon me, but is a white gown the correct thing for the theater, except in a box, for I see our young friend is radiant to-night as snow."

"No," answered Ethel, very positively, "it is the worst possible form, and if we were going in the same party, I should not hesitate to ask Miss Corbin to wear something quieter. Otherwise we would all be made conspicuous from her bad judgment."

Miss Maywood had on her darkest and severest tweed frock, and her most uncompromising turban. Mr. Romaine, having got this much out of Miss Maywood, proceeded to extract amusement from Miss Corbin. He went over to her, and leaning down, whispered:

"My dear young friend, I wish you had persuaded Miss Maywood into wearing something more festive than her traveling gown on this occasion. Because ladies wear their bonnets at the theater, that is no reason why they should ransack their trunks for their oldest and plainest gowns, too."

"I quite agree with you," answered Letty, promptly, who was not ill-pleased to be complimented at Ethel Maywood's expense. "She looks a regular guy. Of course if we were going together, I should n't mind giving her a delicate hint, because it would scarcely be kind of me to carry off all the honors of costume on the occasion, and no doubt she would be much obliged to me. But I really can't interfere now."

Mr. Romaine went off chuckling, and the whole way to the theater he was evidently in a state of suppressed amusement, which puzzled Ethel very much.

Arrived in their seats, which were near the other party, Letty settled herself with an ecstatic air of enjoyment to hear the play. The overture was unmixed delight. So was the first quarter of the first act. But in about ten minutes "the fun began," as Farebrother afterward ruefully expressed it. The play was one of the larkiest descriptions of larky French comedy.

At the first *risqué* situation, Farebrother, whose heart was in his mouth, saw the Colonel's eyes flash, and an angry dull red creep into his fine old face. Letty was blissfully unconscious of the whole thing, and remained so much longer than the Colonel. But when the

curtain came down on the first act, her cheeks
were blazing, and she turned a pair of indignant eyes full on Farebrother, who felt like a
thief, a sneak, and a liar.   What made Letty
blush never frightened her in the least, but
simply angered her, so that she was always
able to take care of herself.   Farebrother, whose
ruddy face was crimson, and who struggled
between a wild disposition to swear and to
laugh, leaned over toward the Colonel, and
said in an agonized whisper, that Letty caught
distinctly:

"For Heaven's sake, Colonel, don't think
that I brought you knowingly to see this
thing.   I had never seen it myself, and merely
went by the advertisement in the papers."

"Your intentions were no doubt good, my
young friend," replied the Colonel, stiffly,
"but you should exercise greater care in the
selection of plays to which you ask innocent
young women."

At that, Farebrother would have been
thankful if the floor had opened and swallowed
him up.   But Letty had evidently heard his
few words of explanation, and they had molli-
fied her.   She felt sorry for Mr. Farebrother,
and pitied his chagrin.

"Nevertheless, sir," continued the Colonel, in a savage whisper, "if this sort of thing continues, I shall deem it my duty to withdraw my granddaughter."

Farebrother was in an agony, and looking around, he saw Mr. Romaine's bright eyes fixed on him gleaming with malicious amusement. Poor Farebrother at that moment was truly to be pitied. But disaster followed disaster, and worse ever seemed to remain behind. The second act was simply outrageous, and Farebrother, although he had more than the average masculine tolerance for *risqué* and amusing plays, was so disconcerted by the Colonel's scowl and Letty's discomfort that he fixed his eyes on his program and studied it as if it were the most fascinating composition he had ever read. Not so the Colonel. He kept his attention closely upon the stage, and at one point which brought down the house with roars of laughter and applause, the Colonel rose, with a snort, and with a countenance like a thunder-cloud, offering his arm to Letty, stalked down the main aisle of the theater, with Farebrother, utterly crestfallen, following them. Not only was Farebrother deeply annoyed at having brought his innocent Virginia friends to such a play, but the absurdity of his own position and the illimitable chaff he would have to put up with on account of it at the club and at masculine dinners was a serious consideration with him.

And there was no room for misunderstanding the reason of their departure. The Colonel's face was a study of virtuous indignation. Letty was crimson, and her eyes persistently sought the floor, particularly as they passed the Romaine party, while poor Farebrother's hangdog look was simply pitiable. He glanced woefully at Mr. Romaine and Dr. Chessingham; both of them were grinning broadly, while a particular chum of his, who had an end seat, actually winked and poked a stick at him as he followed his friends out.

In the carriage he laid his hand upon the knee of the Colonel, who had maintained a terrible and portentous silence, and said, earnestly:

"Pray, Colonel Corbin, forgive me for my mistake in taking you and Miss Corbin there. Of course I did n't dream that anything would be given which would offend you, and I am more sorry than I can express."

The Colonel cleared his throat and responded:

"I can well believe, my dear sir, that your mistake came from the head, not the heart, and as such I fully condone it. But I could not allow my granddaughter to remain and see and hear things that no young girl, or any woman for that matter, should see or hear, and so I felt compelled to take some decisive step. I am prodigiously concerned at treating your hospitable intention to give us pleasure in this manner. But I ask you, as a man of the world, what was I to do?"

Farebrother restrained his inclination to haw-haw at the Colonel's idea of a man of the world, and accepted his view of the whole thing with the most slavish submission. He whispered in Letty's ear, though, as they rattled over the cobblestones, "Forgive me," to which Letty, after a moment, whispered back, "I do."

As it was so early in the evening, Farebrother proposed Delmonico's, not having the courage to suggest any more theaters. They went, therefore, and had a very jolly little supper, during which the *entente cordiale* was thoroughly restored, and the unlucky play forgotten. On the whole the evening did not end badly for Farebrother.

He remained in New York as long as the

Corbins did, which was about two weeks. He accompanied Letty on her shopping tours, aiding her with his advice, which she usually took, and then bitterly reproached him for afterward. When Mrs. Cary's chair had been bought, and lavish presents for Miss Jemima, the Colonel, Dad Davy and all the servants, and an evening gown contracted for, Letty then quite unexpectedly indulged in a full set of silver for her toilet table. This left her without any money to buy the shoes, gloves, and fan for her evening gown, but Letty consoled herself by saying:

"Very probably I sha'n't have a chance to wear it, anyhow, after we get back to the country, and I could n't use white gloves and shoes and a lace fan every day, and I can use a silver comb and brush, and look at myself in a silver glass."

Ethel Maywood thought this very impractical of Letty, and Farebrother laughed so uproariously that Letty was quite offended with him. But she frankly acknowledged that she felt happier after her mind had been relieved of the strain of spending so large a capital, than when she was burdened with its responsibilities. The Colonel's purchases were

very much after the same order.   He bought
a pair of carriage horses which in Virginia he
could have got for considerably less than he
paid, and he quite forgot that the rickety
old carriage for which they were intended
was past praying for.   He also bought a
variety of ornamental shrubs and plants for
which the climate at Corbin Hall was totally
unsuited.   He indulged himself in twelve
dozen of port, which, with his hotel bills, swallowed up the rest of his cash capital.

Meanwhile, Sir Archy was by no means out
of the running, and saw almost as much of his
cousins as Farebrother.   But he became
deeply interested in New York, and went to
work studying the great city with a characteristic English thoroughness.   Before the
two weeks were over, he knew more about
the city government, taxation, rents, values,
commerce, museums, theaters, press, litera-
ture, and everything else, than Farebrother
did, who had lived there all his life.

The night before the Corbins were to start
for Virginia, Letty knocked at the door of the
Chessinghams' sitting-room to say good-by.
Ethel Maywood opened the door for her.   She
was quite alone, and the two girls seated

themselves for a farewell chat. They did not like each other one whit better than in the beginning, but neither had they infringed the armed neutrality which existed between them. They knew that in the country that winter they would be thrown together, and sensible people do not quarrel in the country; they are too dependent on each other.

"And I suppose I am to congratulate you," said Ethel, with rather a chill smile.

"On what, pray?" asked Letty, putting the top of her slipper on the fender, and clasping her hands around her knee in a graceful but unconventional attitude.

"Upon your engagement to Mr. Farebrother," said Ethel, looking more surprised than Letty.

"But I am not engaged to Mr. Farebrother," answered Letty, sitting up very straight, "and he has not asked me to marry him."

"Oh, I am so sorry for you," cried Ethel. "I would never have mentioned it if I had known."

"Why are you sorry for me?" demanded Letty, her cheeks showing a danger signal.

"Because — because, dear, after a man has paid a girl the marked attention for weeks

that Mr. Farebrother has paid you, it is certainly very bad treatment not to make an offer, and I should think your grandpapa would
bring Mr. Farebrother to terms."

Letty's surprise was indescribable. She
could only murmur confusedly :

" Grandpapa — Mr. Farebrother to terms
— bad treatment — what do you mean ? "

" Just what I say," answered Ethel, tartly.
" If a man devotes himself to a girl, he has
no right to withdraw without making her an
offer, and such conduct is considered highly
dishonorable in England."

Rage and laughter struggled together in
Letty's breast, but laughter triumphed. She
lay back in her chair, and peal after peal
of laughter poured forth. Ethel Maywood
thought Letty was losing her mind, until at
last she managed to gasp, between explosions
of merriment, that things were a little different in this country, and that neither she nor
Mr. Farebrother had incurred the slightest
obligation toward each other by their conduct.

It was now the English girl's turn to be
surprised, and surprised she was. In the
midst of it Mr. Romaine came in upon one

8

of his rare visits. He demanded to know the meaning of Letty's merriment, and Letty, quite unable to keep so diverting a cat in the bag, could not forbear letting it out. Mr. Romaine enjoyed it in his furtive, silent manner.

It found its way to Farebrother's ears, who was as much amused as anybody, and when he and Letty met a few hours afterward, each of them, on catching the other's eye, laughed unaccountably.

The Romaine party was to follow later in the season, considerable preparations being necessary for the house at Shrewsbury to be inhabitable after forty years of solitude. Farebrother and Sir Archy had both accepted the Colonel's pressing invitations to pay a visit to Corbin Hall in time for the shooting, and so the parting with Letty was not for long. He and Sir Archy went with them to the station, and Letty found her chair surrounded by piles of flowers, books, and everything that custom permits a man to give to a girl. There was also a very handsome bouquet with Mr. Romaine's card. Letty penned a card of thanks which Farebrother delivered to Mr. Romaine before Miss Maywood. Mr. Romaine, with elaborate gallantry, placed it in his breast pocket, to Miss Maywood's evident discomfiture.

Meanwhile the Corbins were speeding homeward on the Southern train. Letty had enjoyed immensely her first view of the great, big, outside world.

VI

OVEMBER came, that sunny autumn month in lower Virginia, when the changing woods glow in the mellow light, and a rich, blue haze envelops the rolling uplands; when the earth lies calm and soft, wrapped in the golden brightness of the day, or the cloudless splendor of the moon-lit night. The chirp of the partridge was heard abroad in the land, and that was the sign for Farebrother's arrival. An excursion down to Virginia after partridges concealed a purpose on his part toward higher game and a more exciting pursuit.

One day, though, two or three weeks before Farebrother's arrival, the Colonel received a marked copy of a newspaper. It contained the notice of the collapse of a bank in New York, in which the Farebrother family were large stockholders.

Then came a letter from Farebrother tell-

ing the whole story. By far the bulk of their
fortune was gone, but there was still enough
left for his mother and sisters to live comfortably.

"As for myself," he wrote, "without indulging in any cant or hypocrisy, I can say
that the loss of what might have been mine
has great compensations for me. I shall now
be free to pursue my profession of architecture, which I love with the greatest enthusiasm. Formerly I was handicapped by being
thought a rich man, and among my fellows in
my trade it was always against me that I
took money which I did not need. But now
I am upon the same footing as the rest, and I
shall have a chance to pursue it, not as a *dilettante*, but as a working member of a great
profession. I have done some things that
have been commended, and I have got engagements already, although I have not yet
opened an office. But I have taken one in
New York. So, although I suppose no man
ever lost money who did not regret it, I can
say, with great sincerity, that I know of no
man who ever lost it to whom it was so slight
a real loss."

Letty and the Colonel both liked Farebrother's letter; it was so straightforward and manly. The Colonel, with masculine fatuity, had suggested that Sir Archy and Farebrother should time their visit together. The truth was he did not relish the idea of tramping over meadows and through woods after partridges, nor did he think it hospitable to let one of his guests go alone, but two of them could get along very well, so he managed to ask them both at the same time. Neither one liked the arrangement when he found it out, but neither made any opposition.

Farebrother could not quite fathom how Sir Archy and Letty stood toward each other. Sir Archy had not indulged in any demonstrations toward her, except those that were merely friendly. Judged from the American point of view, his attentions were nothing. And to complicate matters, his following the Corbins and the Romaine party to New York might be understood as committing him as much to Miss Maywood as to Miss Corbin. The Chessinghams, Miss Maywood, and even Sir Archy himself regarded that New York trip as a very important and significant affair, and Sir Archy, not forgetting his British caution in love affairs, had at first congratulated

himself that his motive might be supposed to
be either one of the girls.   But upon further
reflection he rather regretted this.   He knew
that Letty attached not the slightest impor-
tance to anything a man might say or do
short of an actual proposal.

But Ethel Maywood was different.   She
was of good family, accustomed to all the re-
strictions of a young English girl, and Chessingham was one of his best friends, so that it
would be peculiarly awkward if his conduct
had given rise to hopes that never could be
realized.

There was no doubt in Sir Archy's mind,
though, that he preferred Letty.   He had
heretofore felt, in all the slight fancies he had
had for girls, a need for the greatest circum-
spection, for he was a baronet with a rent roll,
and as such distinctly an eligible.   But whether
Letty would take him or not, he had not the
remotest inkling.   Sometimes he reasoned
that the mere fact she exempted him to a
certain degree from the outrageous coquetry
she lavished on Farebrother might be a good
sign.   Again, he felt himself hopelessly out
of the race.   As for Miss Maywood, he had
a half acknowledged feeling that if Letty

did not take him Ethel had the next best
claim. Of course he knew she would marry
Mr. Romaine if he asked her. But this did
not shock him, accustomed as he was to the
English idea that there is a grave, moral obligation upon every girl to marry well if she
can, without waiting for further eventualities.

The boat only came to the river landing
twice a week, so that it happened very naturally both Sir Archy and Farebrother stepped
off the steamer one November evening, and
got into the rickety carriage drawn by the
two showy bobtailed horses bought in New
York, over which Dad Davy handled the ribbons. Dad Davy received the guests with
effusion, and apologized for the restlessness
of the horses.

" Dee ain' used ter de ways o' de quality
yit. Quality folks' horses oughter know to
stan' still an' do nuttin'; ole marse say dee
warn't raise' by no gent'mun, an' dee k'yarn'
keep quiet like er gent'mun's kerridge hosses
oughter."

The horses started off at a rattling pace,
and the carriage bumped along at such a
lively rate over the country road that Sir
Archy fully expected to find himself landed
flat on the ground.

"I don't believe this old trap will ever get us to Corbin Hall," he said to Farebrother.

The two men were pleasant enough together, although each wished the other back in New York. Farebrother inquired about Mr. Romaine, and Sir Archy mentioned that the whole party would be down the next week.

It was quite dusk when the ramshackly old coach rattled and banged up to the door of Corbin Hall. The house looked exactly as it had on that November night ten years before, when Sir Archy had made his entry there.

The hall door was wide open, and from it poured the ruddy glow of the fire in the great drawing-room fire-place, and two candles sent a pale ray into the darkness. The Colonel stood waiting to receive them, with Letty and Miss Jemima in the background. When the two men alighted and entered the house, the Colonel nearly sawed their arms off.

"Delighted to see you, my dear young friends," he cried, "and most fortunate and agreeable for us all that you are here together."

The Colonel, in his simplicity, actually believed this. Miss Jemima's greeting and Letty's was not less cordial, and each of the two men would have felt perfectly satisfied under the circumstances but for the presence of the other.

The shabby, comfortable old library looked exactly as it had done ten years before. The identical square of rag carpet was spread over the handsome floor, polished by many decades of "dry rubbin'." Everything in the room that could shine by rubbing did so—for Africans were plentiful still at Corbin Hall. The brass fender and fire dogs, the old mahogany furniture, all shone like looking-glasses.

Miss Letty regulated her conduct toward her two admirers with the most artful impartiality, and both Sir Archy and Farebrother realized promptly that their visit was to be a season of enjoyment, and not of lovemaking —which last is too thorny a pursuit and too full of pangs and apprehensions to be classed strictly under the head of pleasure. Miss Jemima gave them a supper that was simply an epic in suppers—so grand, so nobly proportioned, so sustained from beginning to end. Afterward, sitting around the library fire, they had to hear a good many of the Colonel's stories, with Letty in a little low chair in the corner, her hands demurely folded in her lap, and the fire-light showing the milky

whiteness of her throat and lights and
shadows in her hazel eyes. Letty was very
silent—for, being a creature of caprice, when
she was not laughing and talking like a
running brook, she maintained a mysterious
silence. One slender foot in a black slipper
showed from under the edge of her gown—
the only sign of coquetry about her — for no
matter how much Puritanism in air and manner Letty might affect, there was always one
small circumstance — whether it was her foot,
her hand, or her hair, or the turn of her head,—
in which the natural and incorrigible flirt was
revealed. The evening passed quickly and
pleasantly to all. The Colonel would not
hear of a week being the limit of their visit.
Within a few days the Romaine party would
be at Shrewsbury, and then there would be a
" reunion," as the Colonel expressed it.

When Farebrother was consigned to his
bed-room that night, with a huge four-poster
like a catafalque to sleep in, and a dressing-
table with a frilled dimity petticoat around it,
and the inevitable wood-fire roaring up the
chimney, he abandoned himself to pleasing
reflections, as he smoked his last cigar. How
pleasant, home-like, and comfortable was

everything! Nothing was too good to be
used — and the prevailing shabbiness seemed
only a part of the comfort of it all. And
Letty, like all true women, was more charming in her own home than anywhere else in
the world.

Sir Archy, in the corresponding bed-room
across the hall, with a corresponding catafalque, petticoated dressing-table, etc., likewise
indulged in retrospection before he went to
bed. He was not so easy in his mind — no
man can be at peace who has two women in
his thoughts. He was very sorry the Romaine party were coming. He had not dis-
criminated enough in his attentions between
Letty and Ethel Maywood, and the feeling
that he might be playing fast and loose with
Ethel troubled and annoyed him. But love
with him was a much more prosaic and conventional matter, though not less sincere, than
with Farebrother, who had the American dis-
regard of consequences in affairs of the heart.

Next morning was an ideal morning for
shooting. A white haze lay over the land,
tempering the glory of the morning sun. The
rime lay over the fields just enough to help

the scent of the dogs, and there was a calm, chill stillness in the air that boded ill for partridges.

The Colonel turned his two young friends over to the care of Tom Battercake, and the trio started off accompanied by a good-sized pack of pointers. Sir Archy had on the usual immaculate English rig for shooting— immaculate in the mud and stains necessary for correct shooting clothes. His gun, game-bag, and whole outfit were as complete as if he had expected to be cast ashore on a desert island, with only his trusty weapon to keep him from starvation. Farebrother's gun, too, was a gem—but in other respects he presented the makeshift appearance of a man who likes sport, but does not affect it. His trousers, which had belonged, not to a shooting-suit, originally, but had attended first a morning wedding, were so shabby as to provoke Letty's most scathing sarcasm. His coat and hat were shocking, and altogether he looked like a tramp in hard luck. Tom Battercake, much to Sir Archy's surprise, was provided with an ancient and rusty musket of the vintage of 1840, with which he proposed

to take a flyer occasionally.   Sir Archy privately expressed his surprise at this to Farebrother, who laughed aloud.

"That's all right down here," he said, still
laughing.   "There's game enough for everybody—even the darkeys."

Sir Archy could not quite comprehend this—
but he reflected that not much damage could
be done by such a piece of ordnance as the
old musket.   However, he soon changed his
mind — for Tom, by hook or by crook,
managed to fill a gunny bag which he had
concealed about his person quite as soon
as Sir Archy and Farebrother filled their
bags, and still he gave them all the best
shots.   Sir Archy's wrath was aroused by
some of Tom's unique methods—such as
knocking a partridge over with the long bar-
rel of his musket as the bird was on the
ground, and various other unsportsmanlike
but successful devices.   But there was no
way of bringing Tom's iniquities home to
him, who evidently considered the birds of
the air were to be caught as freely as the
fishes of the sea.   So Sir Archy soon relapsed
into silent disgust.   He was a superb shot,
but Tom Battercake fairly rivaled him, while

Farebrother was a bad third. After tramping about all the morning, they sat down on
the edge of the woods to eat the luncheon
with which Miss Jemima had provided them.
While they were sitting on the ground, Tom
was noticed to be eying Sir Archy's beautiful gun with an air of longing. Presently he
spoke up diffidently, scratching his wool.

"Marse Archy—please, suh—ain' you gwi'
lem me have one shot outen dat ar muskit o'
yourn?"

Sir Archy's first impulse was to throw the
gun at Tom's woolly head, but on reflection he merely scowled at him. Farebrother
laughed.

"There, you rascal," he said, "you may
take my gun, and don't blow your head off
with it."

Sir Archy was paralyzed with astonishment
— not so Tom, who dashed for the gun and
disappeared in the underbrush with Rattler,
the dean of the corps of pointers at Corbin
Hall. In a little while a regular fusillade was
heard, and in half an hour Tom appeared with
a string of partridges on his shoulder, and a
broad grin across his face.

"Thankee, thankee, marster," he said to

Farebrother, returning the gun. "Dat ar muskit o' yourn cert'ny does shoot good. I ain' never shoot wid nuttin' like her — an' ef dis nigger had er gun like dat, ketch him doin' no mo' wuk in bird time!"

Sir Archy forbore comment, but he concluded that American sport, like everything else American, was highly original and inexplicable.

The week passed quickly enough. Every day, when the weather was fine, they went out in the society of Tom Battercake. In the afternoon the lively horses were hitched up to some of the mediæval vehicles at Corbin Hall, and they took a drive through the rich, flat country, Letty being usually of the party. She was surprisingly well behaved, but Farebrother doubted if it was a genuine reform, and suspected truly enough that it was only one of Letty's protean disguises. When the week was out the Colonel would not hear of their departure, and Sir Archy promptly agreed to prolong his visit. Of course, when he decided to stay, Farebrother could not have been driven away with a stick. At the beginning of the second week Mr. Romaine, the Chessinghams and Miss Maywood arrived at

Shrewsbury. Within a day or two the Colonel and Letty, and their two guests, set out one afternoon for Shrewsbury to pay their first call.

Instead of the picturesque shabbiness of Corbin Hall, Shrewsbury was in perfect repair. It was a fine old country house, and when they drove up to the door, it had an air of having been newly furbished up outside and in that was extremely displeasing to the Colonel.

"Romaine is an iconoclast, I see," he remarked, fretfully. "He is possessed with that modern devil of paint and varnish that is the ruin of everything in these days. The place looks quite unlike itself."

"But does n't it look better than it ever did?" asked Letty, who would have been glad to see some paint and varnish at Corbin Hall. This the Colonel disdained to answer.

They were ushered into a handsome and modernly furnished drawing-room by Mr. Romaine's own man, who wore a much injured expression at finding himself in Virginia and the country to boot. Newport suited his taste much better. The Colonel sniffed contemptuously at the Turkish rugs, divans, ottomans,

lamps, screens and bric-à-brac that had taken
the place of the ancient horsehair furniture.
Letty looked around, consumed with envy
and longing.

Presently Mr. Romaine appeared, followed
by the Chessinghams and Ethel Maywood,
who was looking uncommonly handsome. As
soon as greetings were exchanged, the Colonel attacked Mr. Romaine about what he
called his "vandalism" in refurnishing his
house. Mr. Romaine laughed his peculiar
low laugh.

"Why, if I had let that old rubbish remain
here, which had no associations whatever, except that it was bought by my father's agent
— a person of no taste whatever — I should
have been constantly reminded of the flight of
time, a thing I should always like to forget."

"Life, my dear Romaine," remarked the
Colonel, solemnly, "is full of reminders of
the flight of time to persons of our advanced
years, and we have but a brief span in which
to prepare for another world than this sub-
lunary sphere."

At this Mr. Romaine, excessively nettled,
turned to Letty and began to describe to her
a very larky ballet he had witnessed in New

York just before leaving for Virginia. Letty,
in her innocence, missed the point of the story,
which annoyed and amused Mr. Romaine.
The Colonel by that time was deep in conversation with gentle Gladys Chessingham,
whom he sincerely admired, and so did not
catch Mr. Romaine's remarks, of which he
would have strongly disapproved.

Among the four young people—Farebrother, Letty, Sir Archy and Ethel Maywood—a slight constraint existed. Each girl
so resolutely believed in the falsity of the
other's ideas where men were concerned that
each was on the alert to be shocked. Sir
Archy was wondering if his friends, the Chessinghams, were suspecting him of trifling with
Ethel Maywood's feelings, and Farebrother
was heartily wishing that Ethel would succeed
in landing the baronet in her net, and so leave
Letty for himself.

Nevertheless, they made talk naturally
enough. Ethel was secretly much disgusted
with the country as she saw it. There were
few of the resources of English country life at
hand, and as she had been educated to de-
pending upon a certain round of conventional
amusements to kill time, she was completely

at a loss what to do without them. Reading
she regarded as a duty instead of a pleasure.
But with the class instincts of a well born
English girl, she conceived it to be her duty
to say she liked the country at all times, and
so protested in her pretty, well-modulated
voice. Sir Archy and Farebrother were temporary resources, but no more. As for Sir
Archy, she regarded him as much more unat-
tainable than he fancied himself to be. It
would be too much good luck to expect for
her to return to England as Lady Corbin of
Fox Court, and so she dismissed the dazzling
vision with a sigh, and made up her mind to
fly no higher than Mr. Romaine. Letty wondered how the domestic machinery ran at
Shrewsbury, with black servants picked up
here and there in the country—for the
Shrewsbury negroes, having no personal ties
to the place, had scattered speedily after the
war. Ethel soon enlightened her.

" Turner "—that was their maid—" is really
excessively frightened at the blacks. They
grin at her so diabolically, and she can't get
rid of the impression that all blacks are can-
nibals, and as for Dodson and Bridge"—the
two valets — "they do nothing but complain to

Reggie, and he says he expects them both to give warning before the month is out."

" I should think they would," cried Letty, laughing, and realizing the woes of two London flunkies in a domestic staff made up of Virginia negroes.

" None of them can read a written order," continued Miss Maywood, who usually avoided the bad form of talking about servants, but who found present circumstances too overpowering for her. " The cook seems an excellent old person, not devoid of intelligence, although wholly without education—and as Reggie liked her way of preparing an omelette, I sent for her to write down the recipe. She came in, laughing as if it were the greatest joke in the world, called me 'honey' and 'child,' and I never could get out of her— although she talked incessantly in her peculiar patois—what I really wished to know."

This amused Sir Archy very much, who went on to relate his experiences with Tom Battercake.

But Mr. Romaine seemed to find Letty more than usually attractive, and soon established himself by her with an air of proprietorship that ran both Sir Archy and Farebrother out of the field altogether. He put on his sweetest manner for her; his fine black eyes grew more and more expressive, and he used upon her a great deal of adroit flattery which was not without its effect. He gave her to understand that he considered her quite a woman of the world. This never fails to please an ingénue, while it is always wise to tell a woman of the world that she is an in- génue. Letty really thought that her visit to Newport and her week or two in New York had made another girl of her. So it had, in one way. It had taught her a new manner of arranging her hair, and several schemes of personal adornment, and she had seen a few pictures and some artistic interiors. But Letty was a girl of robust and well-formed character before she ever saw anything of the outside world at all, and she was not easily swayed by any mere external influences; but she was acutely sensitive to personal influences, and she felt the individual magnetism of Mr. Romaine very strongly. Sometimes she positively dis- liked him, and thought he affected to be young, although nobody could say he was frivolous—and thought him hard and cynical and generally unlovely. But to-day she found

him peculiarly agreeable — he artfully complimented her at every turn — he was unusually
amusing in his conversation, and in fact laid
himself out to please with a power that he
possessed, but rarely exerted. He had seen
in the beginning that Letty was prejudiced
against regarding him as a youngish man, and
this piqued him. He did not pretend, indeed,
to be young, but he decidedly objected to be
shelved along with the Colonel and other fos-
sils — and as for Miss Jemima, who was a few
months younger than himself, he treated her
as if she had been his great-grandmother.
This, however, did not disturb Miss Jemima's
placidity in the least.

The visit was a long one, and it was quite
dark before the ramshackly carriage rattled
out of the gate toward Corbin Hall. Mr.
Romaine had made them all promise to come
again soon, and when they were out of hearing, Letty expressed an admiration for him
which filled Farebrother with a sudden and
excessive disgust.

VII

IR ARCHY and Farebrother remained three weeks at Corbin Hall, and in that time a great many things happened.

There was constant intercourse between the two places, Corbin Hall and Shrewsbury, which were only four miles apart. Neither of the young men made anything of walking over to Shrewsbury for a little turn, nor did the Chessinghams and Miss Maywood consider the walk to Corbin Hall anything but a stroll. Not so Letty, who was no great walker, but a famous rider. Nor did Mr. Romaine, who had a very stylish trap and a well set-up iron-gray riding nag that speedily learned his way to Corbin Hall. Mr. Romaine got to coming over with surprising frequency, much to Miss Maywood's disgust. The Colonel took all of Mr. Romaine's visits to himself, nor was Mr. Romaine ever able to convince him

that Letty was his objective point. As for
Letty, she was a little amused and a little annoyed and a little frightened at the attentions
of her elderly admirer. She did not know in
the least how to treat him — and he had so
much acuteness and finesse, and subtlety of
all sorts, that he had the distinct advantage
of her in spite of her native mother wit. All
her skill was in managing young men — a
youngish old man was a type she had never
come across before — as, indeed, Mr. Romaine
was, strictly speaking, *sui generis*. He was
never persistent — he paid short and very entertaining visits. He made no bones of letting Miss Jemima see that he regarded her as
at least thirty years older than himself. Men
hug the fond delusion that they never grow
old — women live in dread of it — and men are
the wiser.

Ethel Maywood, though, was cruelly disappointed. She thought Mr. Romaine was in
love with Letty, and in spite of that vehement
protest Letty had made at their very first
meeting, she did not for one instant believe
that Letty would refuse so much money. For
Ethel's part, she sincerely respected and admired Mr. Romaine; she had got used to his

peculiarities, and had fully made up her mind to be a good wife to him if Fate should be so kind as to give her a chance. And now, it was too exasperating that Letty, whom she firmly believed could have either Farebrother or Sir Archy, should rob her of her one opportunity. It turned out though that Miss Maywood was mistaken, and Letty did not by any means enjoy the monopoly with which she was credited.

Chessingham, in consequence of the liberal salary paid him by Mr. Romaine, had agreed to remain with him by the year — and, of course, Mr. Romaine had nothing to do with Chessingham's womankind, who elected to stay, to which Mr. Romaine very willingly agreed. Still, the chance of Miss Maywood being some day Mrs. Romaine was not without its effect upon both the young doctor and his pretty wife. But shortly after their arrival at Shrewsbury, they all became convinced that this hope was vain.

One stormy November day, when they had been in Virginia about a fortnight, Mr. Romaine shut himself up in the library as he usually did, and there he remained nearly all day, writing busily. It was too disagreeable

for him to go over to Corbin Hall, which he had
done with uncommon frequency. In fact, every
time he went out to drive or ride he either
said or hinted that he was going over there —
but he did not always go. Mr. Romaine, who
could pay like a prince for other people, and
who treated the Chessinghams magnificently
as regards money, delighted in sticking pins
in the people he benefited — and it must be
acknowledged that much of his attention to
Letty Corbin came from a malicious pleasure
he took in teasing Miss Maywood. After
these announcements as to where he was going, Mr. Romaine would go off, generally on
horseback, his back looking very young and
trim, while his face looked white and old and
bloodless; but as often as not he turned his
horse's head away from Corbin Hall as soon
as he was out of sight of his own windows.
He would grin sardonically at the injured air
Ethel would wear upon these occasions.

But on this day he saw no one, and went
nowhere. About five o'clock, when dusk had
fallen, a message came. Mr. Romaine desired
his compliments to Miss Maywood and Mr.
Chessingham, and would they come to the
library.

The message surprised them both—nevertheless they went with alacrity. Mr. Romaine was walking up and down the luxurious room with a peculiarly cheerful smile, and his black eyes glowing. A single large sheet of paper, closely written, lay on the library table.

"Thank you for coming," he said, in his sweetest tones to Ethel. "I will detain you but a moment. I have been engaged in what is generally a lugubrious performance—making my will. It is now done, and I desire you and Chessingham to witness it."

It gave a slight shock to both of them. Chessingham had always found Mr. Romaine firmly wedded to the idea that, although he was full of diseases, he would never die. He made plans extending onward for twenty, thirty, and even forty years, and although he was decidedly a valetudinarian, he indicated the utmost contempt for his alleged ailments when it came to a serious question. Miss Maywood felt that all her hopes were dashed to the ground. A man who is thinking about getting married does not make his will before that event. She paled a little, but being a philosophic girl, and not being in love with Mr. Romaine, she maintained her composure fairly well. "I wish to read it to you," said he, and then, placing a chair for Ethel, and toying with his *pince-nez*, he continued, with a smile :

"It may astonish you — wills generally do surprise people. But, after all, mine will be found not so extraordinary. I make a few bequests, and then I — make — Miss — Letty — Corbin — my — residuary — legatee."

Mr. Romaine said this very slowly, so as not to miss its dramatic effect. He achieved all he wanted. Ethel flushed violently, and fell back in her chair. Chessingham half rose and sat down again. None of this was lost on Mr. Romaine, who could not wholly conceal his enjoyment of it. He began, in his clear, well-modulated voice, to read the will. It was just as he said. He gave a thousand dollars here, and a thousand dollars there, he left Chessingham five hundred dollars to buy a memento, and then Letty Corbin was to have the rest.

"And now," said he, gracefully handing a pen to Miss Maywood, "will you kindly attest it?"

In the midst of Chessingham's natural disappointment and disgust, he could scarcely refrain from laughing. The whole thing was so characteristic of Mr. Romaine. Ethel felt like flinging the pen in his face, but she was obliged to sign her name, biting her lips as she did so, with vexation. Chessingham's signature followed. Then both of them went out, leaving Mr. Romaine apparently in a very jovial humor.

As soon as they reached their own sitting-room, where Mrs. Chessingham was waiting, devoured with curiosity, Ethel dissolved into tears of anger and disappointment.

"He has made a fool of me," she sobbed, to Chessingham's attempted consolation.

"Who is it that Mr. Romaine can't make a fool of, when he tries?" asked Chessingham, grimly.

"I think," said Mrs. Chessingham, who had much sound sense, "Mr. Romaine acts the fool himself. He has a plenty of money, fairly good health in spite of his imagination to the contrary, and a great deal to make him happy. Instead of that, he is about as dissatisfied an old creature as I ever knew."

"Right," answered Chessingham, "and, Ethel, I am not at all sure that you have n't made a lucky miss."

"That may be," said Ethel, drying her eyes, "but all the same, everybody expected him to offer himself to me. When we left England it was considered, you remember, by all the people we knew, that it was as good as an engagement. And now — to have to go back —" here Ethel could say no more.

"And Letty Corbin — who, I believe, really dislikes him," said Mrs. Chessingham.

"Don't be too sure about Letty," remarked Chessingham. "It 's just as likely as not that he will make another will to-morrow. All this may be simply to enliven the dulness of the country, and to give Ethel warning that she is wasting her time. You notice, he exacted no promise of us — he probably wants us to tell this at Corbin Hall. *I* sha'n't oblige him, for one."

"Nor I," added Ethel. "And one thing is certain, I shall go back to England. I am missing all my winter visits by staying here, and I may not be able to make a good arrangement for the season in town — so I think I shall go."

Both Chessingham and his wife thought this a judicious thing. Ethel was twenty-seven and had no time to lose, and she was clearly wasting it buried in the country — or rather in the wilderness, as she considered it. And, besides, the Chessinghams were fully convinced that Mr. Romaine would not stay long at Shrewsbury. It was a mere freak in the beginning, and they already detected signs of boredom in him.

Within a few days Chessingham mentioned to him casually that Miss Maywood would return to England at the first convenient opportunity. Mr. Romaine received the news with a sardonic grin and many expressions of civil regret.

"My dear Miss Maywood," he said, the next time he ran across her, "you cannot imagine what a gap your absence will make to me. However, since your decision is made, all I can do will be to provide as far as possible for your comfort during your journey back to England. I will even let Chessingham off to take you to New York, and every day, while you are at sea, I will arrange that you shall have some reminder of those that you have left behind in Virginia."

"Thank you," stiffly responded the practical Ethel, who thought that Mr. Romaine had behaved like a brute.

The news of her impending departure was
conveyed to Letty one afternoon when the
two girls were sitting comfortably over Letty's
bedroom fire — for although there was still
no love lost between them, they found no
difficulty in maintaining a feminine *entente cordiale*.   Letty was surprised and said so.

"Of course," said Ethel, who could not
banish her injuries from her mind, "it will
be embarrassing to go back.   Some malicious people will say that Mr. Romaine has
jilted me — but there is not a word of truth
in it."

"Certainly not," cried Letty, energetically.
"Who on earth would believe that you would
marry that old — pachyderm?"   Letty hunted
around in her mind for an epithet to suit Mr.
Romaine, but could think of nothing better
than the one she used.

"I'm afraid plenty of people will believe
it," answered Ethel, with a faint smile — and
then the womanish incapacity to keep a secret
that is not bound by a promise made her tell
Letty the very thing she had declared she
would not tell her.

"It sounds rather ungrateful of you to talk
that way, for Mr. Romaine intends conferring

10

a very great benefit — the greatest benefit — on you."

"What do you mean?" asked the surprised Letty.

"Only this. A week or two ago he called Reggie and me into the library one afternoon, and there lay his will on the library table — and he asked us to act as witnesses and read us the will — and you are — "

Ethel paused a moment. Letty was leaning forward deeply interested.

"Did he leave me money for a pair of pearl bracelets?" she cried.

"No. He made you his residuary legatee, after giving away a few thousand dollars to other people," answered Ethel.

Letty was quick of wit, and took in at once what Ethel meant. Mr. Romaine had left her his fortune.

She grew a little pale and lay back in her chair. Her first feelings were full of contradictions, as her emotions always were where Mr. Romaine was concerned. Money was a delightful thing — she had found that out — but Mr. Romaine's money! And sometimes she hated Mr. Romaine, and laughed at him behind his back — and now she would have to be very attentive to him, and to let him see that she felt her obligations to him. While this was passing through her mind in a chaotic way, she suddenly remembered to ask:

"Did Mr. Romaine authorize you to tell me this?"

"Not exactly," said Ethel. "But he said nothing about keeping it secret, and Reggie says he is convinced Mr. Romaine wishes us to mention it — for he is a very secretive man usually, and never omits any precaution when he wishes a thing kept quiet."

Letty remained strangely still and silent. She was staggered by what Ethel told her, and thoroughly puzzled — and she had a vague feeling that Mr. Romaine had taken an unwarrantable liberty with her.

"I think," said Ethel, "that he wants to marry you, and he imagines this will incline you to him."

"In that case," replied Letty, rising with dignity, "Mr. Romaine makes a very great mistake. Nothing on earth would induce me to marry him."

Ethel did not stay long after this, and Letty was left alone.

Sir Archy and Farebrother had not yet returned from their day's sport. Letty knew that her grandfather would be likely to be sitting alone in the library, and the impulse to tell him this strange and not wholly pleasing thing took hold of her. She ran down-stairs rapidly, opened the door, and there, in the dusky afternoon, dozing before the fire, was the Colonel, with a volume of Goldsmith open upon his knee.

Letty went up to him and touched him gently.

"Grandpapa," she said.

"I was not asleep, my dear," answered the Colonel, very promptly, without waiting for the accusation.

"If you were," said Letty, with nervous audacity, "what I 'm about to tell you will wake you up."

She hesitated for a moment, in order to convey the news in a guarded and appropriate manner — and then, suddenly burst out with —

"Grandpapa — Mr. Romaine has made his will and left me nearly all his money."

The Colonel fairly jumped from his chair. He thought Letty had lost her mind.

"He has, indeed," she continued, in a half-stifled, half-laughing voice. "He read his will to Ethel Maywood and Mr. Chessingham, and got them to sign it as witnesses."

The Colonel could do nothing but gasp for a few moments. Then he lapsed into an amazed silence — his shaggy brows drawn together, and his deep-set eyes fixed on Letty's agitated face.

"And there is something else Ethel Maywood said," kept on Letty, with her face growing scarlet, "something that made me very angry with Mr. Romaine, and I don't like him, anyhow," she said.

"Go on," commanded the Colonel, in a tragic basso.

"She thinks—that—that—Mr. Romaine wants to m—m—marry me—and he fancies this will win me over," said Letty, faintly.

"The old ass!" bawled the Colonel, for once roused out of his placid dignity. "Excuse me, my love, but this is simply too preposterous! When you first spoke, I assure you, I was alarmed—I was actually alarmed —I thought you did not know what you were saying. But, on reflection, knowing, as I do, Romaine's perverse and peculiar character, I can wholly believe what you tell me."

The Colonel paused a moment, and then the same idea that occurred to Chessingham came to him.

"And the making of a will does n't mean the enjoyment of the property, my love. Romaine may have a passion for making wills—some rich men have—and this may be one of a dozen he may make."

Letty said nothing. Money was the greatest good fortune in the eyes of the world—but the scheme devised for her eventual enrichment had serious drawbacks. Mr. Romaine might live for twenty years—even Mr. Chessingham himself did not know precisely what were the old gentleman's real maladies, and what were his imaginary ones — and that would mean twenty years of subservience on her part toward a man for whom she now felt a positive repulsion. She caught herself wishing that Mr. Romaine would die soon — and was frightened and ashamed of herself. And now Mr. Romaine's relatives would hate her!

"All of the Romaine people will hate me," she said, with pale lips, to the Colonel — they were both standing up now before the fire, and although the ruddy blaze made the room quite light, it was dark outside.

"Yes," answered the Colonel, gloomily, "and they may claim undue influence on your part, and then there may be a lawsuit and the devil to pay generally. Excuse my language, my dear."

The Colonel was completely shaken out of his usual composure, and expressed himself in what he was wont to call — " the vulgar — the excessively vulgar tongue." "I foresee a peck of trouble ahead," he continued.

"One thing is certain," said Letty, raising her eyes, "I feel that I hate Mr. Romaine — and with that feeling, I ought not in any event to take his money. And if, as you say, he is merely amusing himself at my expense, and trying to annoy his family, and — and — Ethel Maywood and the Chessinghams, I hate him worse than ever."

"If such is your feeling, you undoubtedly should protest against Romaine's action."

Then there was a commotion in the hall. Farebrother and Sir Archy and Tom Battercake had got home, and there was a rattle of guns on the rack, and Tom Battercake was guffawing over the contents of the game bags.

Both Letty and the Colonel had plenty of

self-possession, and no one during the evening would have suspected that anything out
of the common had occurred.   But Letty went
to bed early and lay awake half the night,
while her dislike for Mr. Romaine grew like
Jonah's gourd.

Next morning, as soon as the coast was
clear, the Colonel sent for Letty into the
library.

" I want to say to you, my love," he began
at once, " that I believe this thing that Romaine has done is not done in good faith.   He
is the sort of man to leave his property to
perpetuate his name in a library or something
of that kind.   And, moreover, if he should
even be in good faith, his relations are not the
people to let so much money go to a compara-
tive stranger without a struggle.   They have
been looking to him now, for two generations,
to set them on their feet, and they will be in-
furiated with you.   And they will have just
cause—for, after reflection, I am convinced
that grave injustice will be done if this money
comes to you.   Then, your personal dislike —"

" Personal dislike ! say personal hatred ; for
I assure you I have felt something more than

mere dislike ever since I heard of this. Queer,
is n't it ? "

" Not at all," replied the Colonel, with the
ghost of a smile. " Your amiable sex is subject to aberrations of that description. However, I think, on the whole, that nothing but
trouble will result if this plan of Romaine's is
carried out — and I would be glad to see
it prevented."

The Colonel had no more idea of the practical value of money than a baby. Nor had
Letty much more — and besides, she had youth
and beauty and *esprit*, and so had managed to
get on very well so far without a fortune.
The Colonel's views decided her.

" Then, grandpapa, the best thing to do
seems to me to be the most direct and straightforward thing. Write to Mr. Romaine and tell
him frankly what we have heard, and say that
I prefer not to incur the obligation he would
lay upon me."

" Precisely what I desired you to say," replied the Colonel, highly gratified.

It required both of them to compose the
letter to Mr. Romaine, but at last it was finished, copied off in the Colonel's best clerk-
like hand with a quill pen, and sealed with his

large and flamboyant seal. This was the letter :

CORBIN HALL, November 21, 18—

MY DEAR ROMAINE:

Circumstances of a peculiar character necessitate this communication on my part, and I am constrained to approach you in regard to a subject on which otherwise I would observe the most punctilious reticence. This refers to certain testamentary intentions on your part concerning my granddaughter, which she and I have heard through direct and responsible sources. Many reasons influence my granddaughter in desiring me to say to you, that with the keenest sense of the good will on your part toward her, and with assurances of the most profound consideration, she feels compelled to decline absolutely the measures you have devised for her benefit. Of these many reasons, I will give only one, but that, my dear Romaine, will be conclusive. It would be a very flagrant wrong, I conceive, to those of your own blood, who might justly expect to be the beneficiaries of your bounty, to find themselves passed over in favor of one who has not the slightest claim of any kind upon you. This would place my granddaughter in a most painful position, and might result in legal complications extremely embarrassing to a delicate minded person of the gentler sex. She begs, therefore, through this medium, that you will change your kind intentions toward her and not bestow upon her that to which she apprehends others are better entitled than herself. With renewed assurances of respect and regard, believe me to be, my dear Romaine,

Your friend and well-wisher,

ARCHIBALD CORBIN.

This, which both the Colonel and Letty thought a grand composition, was despatched to Shrewsbury by Tom Battercake. Tom returned within an hour or two, with a missive. The Colonel sent for Letty to the library to read it. It was written with a fine pointed pen, upon delicately tinted paper with a handsome crest. It ran thus:

Nov. 21.

DEAR CORBIN:
  You always were the most impractical man about money I ever knew. I shall do as I please with my own.
  Yours truly,
  RICH. ROMAINE.

"Most curt and unhandsome," cried the Colonel, flushing angrily. "What does he take me for? I shall at once express my sentiments in writing regarding this extraordinary communication from Romaine."

"No, grandpapa," cried Letty, who agreed with the Colonel in thinking Mr. Romaine's letter extremely impertinent, "I 'll answer it."

Once in a while Letty had her way, and this was one of the occasions. She sat down at the library table, and, with the angry blood mantling her face, dashed off the following to Mr. Romaine.

" Just listen to this, if you please," she cried,
flourishing her pen in dangerous proximity to
the Colonel's nose. " I think Mr. Romaine
will find that he has got a Roland for his
Oliver."

Then, in a melodramatic voice, she read:

My Dear Mr. Romaine:

As you say, you have a right to do as you please with
your own. This personal liberty pertaining to you likewise pertains to me — and I decline positively to be benefited against my will. I will not have your money. Pardon me if I have copied your own brevity and positiveness
in settling this question. I am,

Very truly yours,

Letty Corbin.

The Colonel chuckled over this letter; nevertheless it was against his code to send it,
but Letty was firm, and Tom Battercake was
despatched for the second time that day to
Shrewsbury, with an important communication.

Letty was radiant with triumph. It was
no mean victory to achieve over Mr. Romaine.

" And if he reads between the lines he will
see that he won't be here with those sharp
black eyes and that cackling laugh of his when

it comes to disposing of his property," she gleefully remarked to the Colonel.

But her triumph only lasted until Tom Battercake's return. He brought the following letter from Mr. Romaine:

MY DEAR MISS CORBIN:

Your spirited and delightful letter has just been received. Permit me to say that I have been so charmed with your disinterestedness and freedom from that love of money which is the cancer of our age, that it only determines me the more to allow my well-considered will to stand. I need only make the alteration of leaving the property in trust for you, so that it will be out of your power to dispose of the principal, even to give it to my relatives — whom I particularly do not desire to have it. All I ask is that you continue to me the kindness you have always shown me. My ailments become daily more complicated and acute, but still I possess great vitality, and I would be deceiving you if I gave you to understand that you would not have long to wait for your inheritance. But whether you treat me well or ill, it and myself are both

Forever yours,

RICH. ROMAINE.

At the conclusion of the reading of this letter Letty sat down and cried as if her heart would break, from pure spite and chagrin at Mr. Romaine's "outrageous behavior," as she and the Colonel agreed in calling it.

VIII

R. ROMAINE had certainly succeeded perfectly in a pastime dear
to his heart — setting everybody by
the ears. Colonel Corbin was deeply offended
with him, and made no secret of it.

"For, if the time should come," he said,
with dignity, to Letty and Miss Jemima, "that
Romaine's relations may accuse us of playing
upon Romaine and getting his money out of
him, I desire to be able to prove that we were
not on terms with him. Therefore, I shall
only treat him with the merest civility. I
shall certainly not go to Shrewsbury, and I
trust he will not come to Corbin Hall."

Futile hope! Mr. Romaine came twice as
often as he had ever done before, and the
Colonel and Letty found it practically impossible to freeze him out. Meanwhile, another
complication came upon Letty, who seemed
destined to suffer all sorts of pains and penal-

ties for what are commonly counted the good
things of life. She had privately determined
that it would take all her diplomatic powers
to avert an offer from both Sir Archy and
Farebrother — for there was something of
"the fierceness of maidenhood" about her —
and she was not yet beyond the secret liking
stage with Farebrother, whom she infinitely
preferred. But it dawned upon her gradually
that Farebrother himself was an adept in the
art of walking the tight rope of flirtation. He
would talk to Letty in the rainy days, when he
could not get out of doors,. by the hour, in
such a way that Letty's heart would be in her
mouth for fear the inevitable offer would come
in spite of her. But after a while she discovered that Farebrother could look down without
flinching from the dizzy height of sentimental
badinage, and then quietly walk away. In a
little while these tactics of his bore fruit.
Letty, from being very much afraid that he
would propose, began to be very much piqued
that he did not propose. Kindness was then
lavished upon him — sweet looks on the sly,
and every encouragement was given him to
make a fool of himself, in order that Letty
might be revenged on him. But Farebrother

declined to accept the invitation. He was
shrewd enough to see that Letty's design in
leading him on was simply to throw him over
—and he had no intention to be slaughtered to
make a coquette's holiday. And he knew besides that Letty had a heart—that she was a
·perfect specimen of the Southern type, which
coquettes with the whole world, only to make
the most absolute surrender to one man—
and that her heart was not to be won by letting her make a football of his.

The two men watched each other stealthily,
but Farebrother, in quickness of resource, had
much the advantage of Sir Archy. And he
was clear sighted enough to see that there was
something wrong between the Corbins and
Mr. Romaine. All at once the Colonel and
Letty ceased going to Shrewsbury, and once
when he suggested casually to Letty that they
ride over to see the Chessinghams and Miss
Maywood, the Colonel interfered, with a flush
upon his wrinkled face.

"I would prefer, my dear Farebrother," he
said, "that my granddaughter should not go
to Shrewsbury at present. Rest assured that
my reason is a good one—else I would not
commit so grave a solecism toward a guest in

my house as to object to her going anywhere with you."

Farebrother was completely puzzled — the more so that the objection was all on the Colonel's side — for Mr. Romaine had been at Corbin Hall the day before alone, and the day before that with Chessingham's womankind. He had noticed some slight constraint on Letty's part, but the Colonel had been absent both times. He said no more about going to Shrewsbury, and privately resolved to go there no more except for a farewell visit. This gave him distinctly the advantage over Sir Archy, whose long intimacy and real friendship with Chessingham made it natural and inevitable that he should go often to Shrewsbury.

Letty, however, was no more capable of keeping an unpledged secret than Ethel Maywood, and one afternoon, walking through the pine woods with Farebrother, the whole story about Mr. Romaine and his will came out.

Farebrother sat down on a fallen log and shouted with laughter.

" The old imp ! " he cried, and laughed the more.

" Of course," said Letty, laughing in spite

of herself, "I really don't believe it is in earnest.   Grandpapa says people who make their
wills so openly commonly have a passion for
making wills, and he has no doubt Mr. Romaine is merely doing this for some present
object."

"Certainly," cried Farebrother, laughing
still.   "It 's his own peculiar Romainesque
way of giving Miss Maywood warning.   Pray
pardon me for hinting such a thing, but Miss
Maywood herself has acted with such delicious
candor about the whole matter that it 's absurd to pretend ignorance.   Now what a devilish revenge the old Mephistopheles took!"

Farebrother seemed so carried away by his
enjoyment of Mr. Romaine's tactics in giving
Miss Maywood the slip that Letty was quite
offended with him for his lack of interest in her
side of the case.   But at last he condescended
to be serious.   It was a soft and lovely autumn afternoon, the red sun slanting upon the
straggling woods, and making golden vistas
through the trees.   It was hushed and still.
It had rained that day, and the air was filled
with the aromatic odor of the dead, wet leaves.
Farebrother had remained seated on the log
to have his laugh out, but Letty had got up

and was standing over him in an indignant
attitude, one hand thrust in the pocket of her
natty jacket, while with the other she grasped
firmly the brim of her large black hat, under
which her eyes shone with a peculiar, soft
splendor. Farebrother thought then that he
had never seen her pale, piquant beauty to
greater advantage.

"But if you could for one moment take
your mind off Miss Maywood, and consider
my grievances," said she, tartly. "Can you
imagine anything more odious? Here is Mr.
Romaine pretending — for I don't believe it 's
anything but that he is trying to make a fool
of me — pretending, I say, that he means to
leave me a fortune some day — and he is just
perverse enough to ignore any objection I may
make, not only to his plans, but to himself —
for I assure you, I really dislike him, although
I pity him, too. Then suppose he dies and
does leave me the money! You never heard
of such tribes of poor relations as he has, in
your life, and all of them, as grandpapa says,
have counted on Mr. Romaine's money for
forty years. He has one niece — as poor as
poverty, with nine — shoeless — hatless —
shabby children — who has actually conde-

scended to beg for help from him — and what do you think she will say of me when the truth comes out? And there are whole regiments of nephews — and cousins galore — and the entire family are what grandpapa calls 'litigious' — they 'd rather go to law than not — oh, I can shut my eyes and see the way these people will hound me for that money, that after all should be theirs."

Farebrother was grave enough now. He rose and went and stood by her.

" Money, my dear Miss Corbin, is like electricity or steam, or any other great force — it is dangerous when it is unmanageable. However, he said, lightly, " as I 've had to part with some lately, I 've had to call up all the old saws against it that I could think of."

"But I don't believe you are very sorry about your money."

" Sorry? Then you don't know me. I experienced the keenest regret when I discovered that, according to my father's will, I came out at the little end of the horn in the event of disaster, because, as the dear old gentleman said, I was well able to take care of myself. Of course I said the handsome thing — when the crash came—especially to Colonel Corbin,

who would have kicked me out of his house
if I had n't — but I assure you I did n't feel in
spirits for a whole week after the financial
earthquake."

Letty looked at him smiling. She was not
a bad judge of human nature and much
shrewder than she looked, and she read Farebrother like an open book — and liked the
volume.

" But then, your profession ? "

" Oh, yes, my profession. Well, the first
thing that cheered my gloom was when I got
a contract for an eight-story granite business
building. I met on the street that very day
the fellow I told you of once — a clever architect, but who has a wife and an army of children on him, and who always looked at me
reproachfully in the old days when we met —
and I had the satisfaction of telling him that
it was work or starvation with me now — and
he spoke out the thought I had read so often
in his mind before — ' It 's all right now, but
when I saw you driving those thoroughbreds
round the Park, in that imported drag of yours,
and heard of you buying the pick of the pictures
at the exhibition, while I had seven children
to bring up and educate on my earnings, it

did seem deuced hard that you should enter into competition with us poor devils.' So I reminded him that the thoroughbreds and the pictures and a few other things were going under the hammer, and the wretch actually grinned. But I 'll tell you what I have found out lately — that there 's such a thing as good-fellowship in the world. There is n't any among rich men. They are all bent on amusing themselves or being amused. They are so perfectly independent of each other that there is n't any room for sentiment — while among poorer men they are all interdependent. They have to help each other along in pleasures and work, and that sort of thing — and that 's why it is that comradeship exists among them as it cannot exist among the rich."

" I never knew anything about money until that visit to Newport," said Letty, candidly. " We had bills — and when the wheat crop was sold it paid the bills — that is, as far as it would go — for the wheat crop never was quite as much as we expected, and the bills were always a great deal more than we expected. But I found the spending of that money in New York delightful."

"So did I," answered Farebrother. "Never

enjoyed anything more in my life. You had
more actual, substantial fun in spending that
money than my sisters have out of so many
thousands."

"But I think," remarked the astute Letty,
"that it is more the way we show it. Your
sisters are used to money—"

"That 's it—and so it is as necessary to
them as the air we breathe—but as we breathe
air all the time, we are not conscious of any
ecstatic bliss in doing it."

"Perhaps—but, you see, I am bent on enjoyment, and I am bent on showing it as well
as feeling it."

"In short, you are a very wise girl," said
Farebrother, smiling, "and I think it is a pity
that you are so determined on never bestow-
ing so much wisdom and cheerfulness on some
man or other."

"I have never said I would n't."

"Oh, not in words perhaps, but I imagine
a fixed determination on your part to hold on
to your liberty. You may, however, succumb
to the charms of Sir Archy Corbin, of Fox
Court."

Farebrother emphasized the "Sir" and the
"Fox Court" in a way that Letty thought

disagreeable — and how dared he talk so
coolly of her marrying Sir Archy, without one
single qualifying word of regret? And just
as Farebrother intended, his suggestion did
not help her to regard Sir Archy with any
increase of favor.

"There he is now," cried Farebrother, "shall
I make off so as to give him a chance?

Letty was so staggered by the novelty
and iniquity of Farebrother's perfect willingness to give her up to Sir Archy that she
could not recover herself all at once — and the
next thing, Sir Archy had tramped through
the underbush to them, looking wonderfully
handsome and stalwart in his knickerbockers
and his glengarry pulled over his eyes.

If Letty found that Farebrother was always
joking and difficult to reduce to seriousness,
she could find no such fault with Sir Archy.
He was the literal and exact Briton, who took
everything *au sérieux*, and whose humor was
of the broad and obvious kind that prevails in
the tight little island. He was as much puzzled by the status of affairs between Letty and
Farebrother as Ethel Maywood was — and
could hardly refrain sometimes from classing
Letty as a flirt — a word that meant to him

everything base and dishonorable in womankind — for a flirt, from his point of view, was
a girl with a little money, who led younger
sons and rash young officers and helpless cu-
rates to believe that she could be persuaded to
marry one of them, and ended by hooking a
mature baronet, or an elder son, with a good
landed property.

Flirtation on the American plan, merely to
pass away the time, and with no ulterior object whatever, was altogether incomprehensi-
ble to him. And Letty's perfect self-possession! No tell-tale blush, but a look of the
most infantile innocence she wore, when she
was caught in the very act of taking a sentimental walk with a man! The genuine
American girl — not the imitation Anglo-
American formed by transatlantic travel —
was a very queer lot, thought Sir Archy,
gravely.

"Where have you been?" asked Letty, with
an air of authority, which she alternated with
the most charming submissiveness.

"At Shrewsbury," answered Sir Archy.

"Ah, I know — we all know. There 's a
magnet at Shrewsbury."

Now, to be chaffed about a girl, and par-

ticularly a girl like Miss Maywood—to whom
he had undeniably paid certain attentions, was
both novel and unpleasant to Sir Archy, so he
only answered stiffly, "I don't quite understand your allusion."

"Why, Ethel Maywood, of course!" cried
Letty. "Does anybody suppose that you
would go so often to see that wicked old man
at Shrewsbury? or Mrs. Chessingham and
her husband?"

"If you suppose that there is anything more
than friendship between Miss Maywood and
myself, you are mistaken — and the suspicion
would do Miss Maywood great injustice," said
Sir Archy, with dignity.

"Oh, if you think it would hurt Miss Maywood to have it supposed that you are devoted
to her—"

"I did not intend to say that," answered Sir
Archy, who was neither a liar nor a hypocrite,
and who knew well enough how baronets with
unencumbered estates are valued matrimoni-
ally. "I only meant to state, most emphati-
cally, that there is nothing whatever between
Miss Maywood and myself — and justice
requires—"

"Justice — fudge!" cried Letty, with animation; "who ever heard of justice between a man and a woman?"

"I have," answered Sir Archy, sententiously.

"And next, you will be saying that women are bound by the same rules of behavior as men," continued Letty, with pretty but vicious emphasis.

Farebrother looked on without taking any part in the scrimmage, and was infinitely diverted.

"I hardly think I understand you," said Sir Archy, much puzzled.

"I 'll explain then," replied Letty. "I mean this; that a man should be the soul of honor toward a woman—honorable to the point of telling the most awful stories for her—and always taking the blame, and never accusing her even if he catches her at the crookedest sort of things — and giving her all the chicken livers, and the breast of duck, and always pretending to believe her whether he does or not."

"And may I ask," inquired Sir Archy, who took all this for chaff, without crediting in the least the amount of sincerity Letty felt in her code, "may I ask what is exacted of a

woman in her treatment of men, as a return
for all this?"

"Nothing whatever," replied Letty, airily;
"a man has no rights that a woman is bound
to respect — that is, in this glorious land."

"It strikes me that your rule would work
very one-sidedly."

"It's a bad rule that works both ways,"
declared Letty, solemnly.

Sir Archy did not believe a word of all this;
but Farebrother thought that Letty had not
really over-stated her case very much.

Presently they all turned round and walked
home through the purple twilight. The path
led through the woods to the straggling edges
of the young growth of trees on the borders
of a pasture, now brown and bare. A few
lean cattle browsed about — the Colonel spent
a good deal of time and money, as his fathers
had done before him, in getting the grass out
of his fields, and raising fodder for his stock,
instead of letting the grass grow for them to
fatten on — so they were very apt to be lean
for nine months in the year. The path led
across the pasture to the whitewashed fence
that enclosed the lawn. A young moon
trembled in the opal sky. As they walked

along in Indian file they felt their feet sinking
in the soft, rich earth. The old brick house,
with its clustering great trees, loomed large
before them, and a ruddy light from the library
windows shone hospitably. The dogs ran
yelping toward them as they crossed the lawn,
old Rattler giving subdued whines of delight.
The thoughts of both Sir Archy and Farebrother, all the way home, had been how delicious that twilight walk would have been
with Letty, had only the other fellow been
out of it.

When they got in the house there were
letters—the mail only came twice a week,
and Tom Battercake brought the letters and
papers in a calico bag from the postoffice,
eight miles off. Farebrother read his letters
with a scowl. He had meant to stay a few
days longer—in fact, he determined to stay as
long as Sir Archy, if he could—but he discovered that he could not.

"Business," he said—"I am a working
man, you know, and employers and contractors
won't wait—so I shall have to take the boat
to-morrow."

The Colonel and Miss Jemima were profuse
in their regrets—Letty was civil and Sir

Archy was positively gay, when it was fixed that Farebrother should go the next day. Still, the supper table was cheerful. Farebrother had a very strong hope that Letty and Sir Archy never would be able to understand each other enough to enter into a matrimonial agreement; and then, he was determined to show Miss Letty that he was by no means heartbroken at the prospect of leaving her.

None of the men who had admired Letty Corbin understood her so well as Farebrother. The others had paid her court, more or less sincere, but Farebrother, when he became really interested in her, saw that such tactics would never do. Instead, he made it his business to pique her, so artfully that Letty was completely blind to the facts in the case, and her determination was aroused to conquer this laughing, careless, stiff-necked admirer, whose conduct to her was very like her conduct to others. In the first place, the idea that he should come all the way from New York, upon what seemed likely to turn out a purely platonic errand, was, from her point of view, a most iniquitous proceeding. She did not want any man—but she vehemently and

innocently demanded the homage of all. And
when a man calmly retained his heart and his
. reason, while she invited him to lose both,
was in the highest degree exasperating. But
Farebrother absolutely declined presenting his
head to Letty on a charger, even when they
were alone in the great cold drawing-room,
under the pretense of hearing some farewell
waltzes from Letty's fingers, and it seemed
almost unavoidable that he should say something sentimental. He remained obstinately
cheerful, and kept it up until the last.

He had to leave Corbin Hall at five o'clock
in the morning, so Letty, secretly much disgusted with him on account of his callousness,
had to say farewell the night before. The
Colonel would be up the next morning, and
Miss Jemima, to give him breakfast, but Letty
gave no hint of any such intention. They
had a very jolly evening in the library, the
Colonel being in great feather and telling
some of his best stories while he brewed the
family punch bowl full of apple toddy. Miss
Jemima, too, had been induced by the most
outrageous flattery on Farebrother's part to
bring out her guitar, and to sing to them in a
thin, sweet voice some desperately sentimental

songs of forty years before — "Oh No, We Never Mention Her," "When Stars are in the Quiet Skies," and "Ben Bolt." It was very simple and primitive. The two men of the world enjoyed it much more than many of the costliest evenings of their lives, and neither one could remember anything quite like it. The life at Corbin Hall was as simple and quaint as that of the poorest people in the world—and yet more refined, more gently bred, than almost any of the rich people in the world.

At eleven o'clock, Letty rose to go. Farebrother lighted her candle for her from those on the rickety hall table, and escorted her to the foot of the stairs. It really did cost him an effort then to play the cheerfully departing guest. There was no doubt that Letty had been vastly improved by her touch with the outside world. She had learned to dress herself, which she did not know before — and she had learned a charming modesty concerning herself — and she was quite unspoiled. She still thought Corbin Hall good enough for anybody in the world, and although she admired satin damask chairs and sofas and art drapery, she still cherished an affection for

hair cloth and dimity curtains. This ineradicable simplicity of character was what charmed
Farebrother most — she would always retain
a delightful freshness, and she never could
become wholly sophisticated.

"I can't tell you how much I have enjoyed
being here," he said to her, with hearty sincerity, as he stood at the foot of the stairs,
looking up at Letty. She held the candle a
little above her head, and its yellow circle of
flame fell on her pure, pale face — for this
young lady who tried so hard to make fools
of men, had the air, the face, and the soul of
a vestal.

Letty nodded her head gravely.

"Of course you have enjoyed yourself. We
are such an — ahem — agreeable family."

"I should say so! And to get into a community where people won't even talk about
divorce — and where nobody chases the dollar
very hard — and where the dear Colonel is
considered a very practical man — pray excuse
me, Miss Corbin, but I do think your grandfather the noblest old innocent!"

"I know it. Grandpapa *is* innocent. So
is Aunt Jemima. I am the only worldling in
the family."

12

"My dear young friend,— for you must allow me to address you as a father after that astounding statement,— you are not, and never can be worldly minded. You are a very clever girl — but it is the wisdom of the dove, not of the serpent."

"Very graceful indeed. I thank you. You have a pretty wit when you choose to exercise it. Now, good-by. I hope so much I shall, some time or other, see — your sisters — again."

"Oh, hang my sisters! Don't you want to see me again?"

"Y – y – yes. A little. A very little." But while saying this, her hand softly returned Farebrother's clasp.

It was still dark next morning, when Letty slipped out of bed and ran to the window, pulling aside the dimity curtains — she had heard the old carriage rattling up to the door. The moon had gone down, but the stars still shone in the blue black sky. Presently Farebrother came out, accompanied by the Colonel. Letty could hear their voices, and saw Farebrother take off his hat as he shook the Colonel's hand. Then he sprang into the carriage. Tom Battercake gave the restless horses a cut with a long sapling with all the twigs cut off, and in two minutes the rig had disappeared around the turn in the lane. Letty crept back to bed, feeling as if something pleasant had suddenly dropped out of her life. She determined to go to sleep again, and to sleep as late as she could. There was no object in going down to breakfast early — only Sir Archy would be there. Then she began to think about Farebrother — and her last conscious thought was: "A man so hard to get must be worth having."

IX

EANWHILE, a period of convulsion was at hand for the happy family at Shrewsbury. As soon as it was decided that Miss Maywood was to return to England, a number of obstacles arose, as if by magic, to her departure—and they were all inspired by Mr. Romaine. As she was to cross alone he declared that she must do it only under the charge of a certain captain—and when inquiries were made at the steamship office in New York, it turned out that this particular captain had a leave of absence on account of ill health, and would not command his ship again until after Christmas. Mr. Romaine proposed to wait for this event, if it did not occur until midsummer. Then some acquaintances were discovered who intended sailing almost immediately, but Mr. Romaine suddenly grew very ailing, and could not part

with Mr. Chessingham to take his sister-in-
law to New York. Besides he found every
imaginable fault with the proposed traveling
companions, and the Chessinghams and Ethel
felt that, after enjoying Mr. Romaine's hospitality for so long, they ought to defer to him
as regarded the impending departure. Therefore, although Miss Maywood had undoubtedly got her congé from Mr. Romaine, she was
still under his roof well on in December, and
it looked as if he would succeed in doing to
her what Letty complained of in her own case
— making a fool of her. Ethel was really very
anxious to leave; but this reluctance to give
her up on the part of her elderly and eccentric
friend made her wonder sometimes whether,
after all, Mr. Romaine would let her return to
England without him. He openly declared
that he was tired of Virginia and meant to take
a house in London for the season; and he actually engaged, by correspondence, a charming house at Prince's Gate, from the first of
April. Ethel felt that it would be flying in the
face of Providence to insist upon going, as
long as there was a chance of her presiding
over the house in Prince's Gate. And the liberty and spending-money enjoyed by Ameri-

can women seemed daily more pleasing to her. Whatever could be said against Mr. Romaine, his worst enemy could not charge him with meanness. He gave with a princely generosity that made Ethel—who thought that nobody got more than three per cent. interest on money—think he was worth millions. Sir Archy had gone away from Corbin Hall a few days after Farebrother left, but was to return after Christmas; but Ethel put Sir Archy out of her mind altogether—she was eminently reasonable, and never counted upon the vaguely brilliant.

The beginning of more serious upheavals was the announcement, one day, from Bridge, Mr. Romaine's own man, and Dodson, who was also Mr. Romaine's man, but waited on Mr. Chessingham, that they desired to leave at the end of the month; and Carroll, the ladies' maid, gave simultaneous warning.

"I 'ave been, sir, with Mr. Romaine for sixteen year, and I 'ave put hup with 'im, and I could put hup with 'im for sixteen year more; but this stoopid country and the willainous blacks is too much for me," Bridge announced to Chessingham, with an injured air. Dodson followed suit, and Carroll tearfully explained that she 'ad been in mortial terror ever since she first knew the blacks, for fear they would kill and eat her.

Chessingham was secretly much delighted with this, and confided his feelings to his wife and Ethel.

" It will take the old curmudgeon back to London quicker than anything on earth that could have been devised," he said. " He can't get on without Bridge — nobody else, I ' m told, ever stayed with him more than three months — and he 'll be forced to quit."

In the library a characteristic interview was taking place between Bridge and his master. Bridge, feeling like a felon, announced his determination to leave.

" That 's quite satisfactory," remarked Mr. Romaine, raising his black eyes from his book. " I have been thinking for some time that I needed a younger and more active man. I do not like men of any sort when they become antiquated."

Bridge opened his mouth to speak, but dared not. He was at least twenty years younger than Mr. Romaine, and there he was reproached with his age !

However, some faint stirring of the heart

toward the man he had served so long, and
who had given him some kicks, but a good
many ha'pence, too, made him say hesita-
tingly:

"Wot's troublin' me, sir, is how is you goin'
to be hattended to when you're hill; and how
is you to get shaved, sir?"

"As to my attendance when I am ill, that is
a trifle; and shaving will be unnecessary, as I
have intended for some time past to turn out
a full beard," promptly responded Mr. Romaine. "Now you may go. When you are
ready to leave come to me and I will give you
a check."

The idea of Mr. Romaine in a full beard
drove Bridge immediately into the pantry,
where he confided the news to Dodson, and
they both haw-hawed in company.

Nevertheless, the loss of his man, who knew
some secrets about his health, was a very serious one to Mr. Romaine. Also, he had never
shaved or dressed himself in his life, and to
him immaculateness of attire was a necessity.
He turned the ridiculous and embarrassing
question over in his mind — how was he to
get shaved? — until it nearly drove him to asking Bridge to reconsider his decision. But

before doing that, he went over to Corbin Hall one day, where a new solution of the difficulty presented itself.

It was a bright, wintry day in December when he was ushered into the shabby library, where sat the Colonel. Now, although none of the family from Corbin Hall had darkened the doors of Shrewsbury for a month past, Mr. Romaine had calmly ignored this, and had treated the Colonel's studied standoffishness with the most exasperating nonchalance. Colonel Corbin could not be actively rude to any one to have saved his own life, and the extent of his resentment was shown merely in not visiting Mr. Romaine, and receiving him with a stiffness that he found much more difficult to maintain than Mr. Romaine did to endure. The struggle between the Colonel's natural and sonorous urbanity toward a guest and his grave displeasure with Mr. Romaine was desperate; and Mr. Romaine, seeing it with half an eye, enjoyed it hugely. The idea of taking Colonel Corbin seriously was excessively ludicrous to him; and the Colonel's expectation of being taken seriously on all occasions he thought the most diverting thing in the world.

"How d' ye do, Corbin?" said Mr. Romaine, entering with a very jaunty air.

"Good-day, Mr. Romaine," answered the Colonel, sternly — and then suddenly and unexpectedly falling into his habitual tone, he continued, grandiloquently:

"Has your horse been put up, and may we have the satisfaction of entertaining you at dinner?"

"Oh, Lord, no," answered Mr. Romaine, smiling; "I merely came over to see how you and Miss Corbin were coming on — and to ask you a most absurd question."

"My granddaughter is coming on very well. For myself, at my time of life — and yours, too, I may say — there is but one thing to do — which constitutes coming on well — and that is to prepare for the ferriage over the dark river."

"I do not anticipate needing the services of the ferryman for a good while yet, and my heirs, I apprehend, will have a long wait for their inheritance," snapped Mr. Romaine, who was always put in a bad humor by any allusion to his age. Colonel Corbin, though, could not stand Mr. Romaine's hasty allusion to his heirs, and without saying a word, turned away, and with a portentous frown began to stare out of the window.

Mr. Romaine, after a moment or two, cooled down and proceeded to make amends in his own peculiar fashion for his remark.

" Excuse me, Corbin, but you are so devilish persistent on the subject of my age that I inadvertently used an illustration I should not have done had I reflected for one instant whom I was addressing. But I take it that no gentleman will hold another accountable for a few words said in heat and under provocation. Remember, 'an affront handsomely acknowledged becomes an obligation.'"

" Your acknowledgment, sir, was not what I should call a handsome one."

" Hang it, Corbin, we can't quarrel. Here I am in trouble, and I have come to you, as to my friend of forty years, to help me out."

It was always hard for the Colonel to maintain his anger, and Mr. Romaine, when he said this, put on one of his characteristic appealing looks, and spoke in his sweetest voice, and the Colonel could not help relaxing a little.

" I think you understand, Romaine, the attitude I feel compelled to assume toward you;

but — but — if you are really in unpleasant circumstances —"

"Deuced unpleasant, I assure you. I 've had a man for sixteen years — never knew him to make a mistake, to be off duty when required, or to have any serious fault — and now he swears he can't stand Virginia any longer, and intends leaving me in the lurch. I can't stand Virginia much longer myself, but I don't want the villain to know that his loss is actually driving me back to England before my time. But the case is this — I can't shave myself. Does that black fellow of yours, David, shave you?"

"I always shave myself — but David understands the art of shaving, and has practised it on guests upon various occasions, with much success."

"I wish you would send him over to Shrewsbury to-morrow. If I can't get a man by the time Bridge leaves — which will be next week — I might ride over here every day, and, with your permission, make use of David's services until I can get a capable white man."

To say "No" was generally impossible to

the Colonel, so he weakly yielded. He would send David over on the next day.

Mr. Romaine did not ask to see Letty, and went off after a short visit, leaving the Colonel in a very bad humor indeed.

Nevertheless, next day Dad Davy appeared and was introduced into Mr. Romaine's bed-room. Dad Davy was not only honored by being thought capable of shaving Mr. Ro-maine, but he had brought his implements with him in a rusty-looking rush basket.

"You may know that I am about to dismiss my man; and I desired to find out if I could get any sort of a barber, in case there might be delay in the arrival of a man from New York that my agent will send me," said Mr. Romaine. He was sitting in a large chair, with a newspaper in his hand, and wore a flowered silk dressing-gown, and evidently had not been shaved.

"Lord, yes, sir; I kin shave er gent'mun," answered Dad Davy, with visions of a silver quarter illuminating his imagination. "I done brung some new shavin' things wid me, and ef you wuz to let me git de hot water, I kin trim yo' face jes' ez clean ez er b'iled onion."

"Very well; you may try your hand," said Mr. Romaine, picking up his paper. "There is the shaving-table."

Dad Davy tiptoed over to the shaving-table, and examined suspiciously the silver toilet articles, the spirit-lamps, scented soaps, etc., etc. Mr. Romaine, absorbed in his paper, presently heard Dad Davy, in an apologetic tone, saying:

"Marse Richard, I k'yarn do nuttin' wid dem gorgeousome things. I got some mighty good soap here, an' a new shavin'-bresh; an' ef you will jes' lem me took yo' razor—"

"All right," answered Mr. Romaine, deep in his paper.

In a few minutes Dad Davy remarked, "I 'se ready," and Mr. Romaine, lying back in his chair, shut his eyes, while Dad Davy began the lathering process. When it was about half done Mr. Romaine began sniffing suspiciously, but he could not open his mouth. Dad Davy then began with the razor, and a smoother or more luxurious shave Mr. Romaine never had in his life. As soon as he could speak, he growled:

"What infernal soap is that you 've got there?"

"Hi, Marse Richard," answered Dad Davy, in a surprised voice. "I got de bes' kin' o' soap fur shavin'. Dis heah is de bes' sort o' *sof'* soap, made outen beef taller an' ash lye— none o' your consecrated lye, but de drippin's f'um er reg'lar lye gum, full o' hick'ry ashes —an' I brung er go'd full."

Dad Davy produced a large gourd full of a molasses-like substance, which he poked under Mr. Romaine's high-bred nose.

"Good heavens!" yelled Mr. Romaine, jumping up and seizing a towel with much violence.

"Now, Marse Richard, what you gwine on dat way fur? Sof' soap is de bes' fur shavin'. Did n't I gin you er easy shave?"

"Yes, you did—but this villainous stuff— where 's your shaving-brush?"

Dad Davy triumphantly produced a shaving-brush made mop-fashion by tying a mass of cotton threads to a short wooden handle.

"My ole 'oman made dis heah," said Dad Davy, exhibiting this instrument with great pride. "She make 'em fur ole Marse—and dis heah is er bran new one—co'se I war n' goin' use no u'rr but a new one fur you, Marse Richard—"

Mr. Romaine looked in speechless disgust from Dad Davy to the rusty basket, the "go'd" of soap, and the mop for a shaving-brush. But without one word he sat down again, and Dad Davy finished the job in perfect style. Just as he had got through, a tap came at the door, and Bridge entered — and came very near dropping dead in his tracks at the paraphernalia of the new barber. Mr. Romaine was saying affably:

"A most satisfactory shave — the best I 've had for years. I would prefer, however, my own things next time. Give me the bay rum."

Dad Davy soused his client with bay rum, and then taking up the gourd, mop, etc., put them in the basket, and stood, expectant of his quarter.

"Here 's a dollar for you," said Mr. Romaine; "and say to Colonel Corbin I am much obliged for your visit to-day — and if I had as good a barber as you I should not follow his plan of shaving himself."

Dad Davy, although secretly astounded at the magnificence of the gift, disdained to show his delight before "po' white trash," as he regarded Bridge, and making a profound bow, took himself and his basket off.

Bridge, however, after the manner of his kind, seeing his master independent of him, began to reflect that he had a good place and high wages, and that if Mr. Romaine was a difficult master to serve, all masters had their faults; and he finally concluded to stay. He went to Mr. Romaine therefore a few days afterward, and with much shuffling, hemming, and hawing, declared his willingness to remain, provided Mr. Romaine went to England in April. At this Mr. Romaine expressed much surprise, and declared that his return to England was quite problematical and might never occur. Bridge, though, saw unmistakable signs that Mr. Romaine's latest freak had outworn itself, and at last knuckled down completely — when he was restored to favor. Dodson then followed the prevailing wind and asked to be reinstated; and Carroll, the maid, being a diffident maiden of forty, declared she could n't think of traveling alone from Virginia to New York; and so, with the delays attending Miss Maywood's departure, it looked as if the Shrewsbury party would depart intact as when it came.

But a disturbance greater than any that yet occurred was now impending, and was brought about by the innocent agency of Colonel Corbin.

One evening the Colonel had his two fine horses hitched up to a two-wheeled chaise which had been resurrected from the loft of the carriage-house during the emergencies of the war time, and started out for the river landing for a parcel he expected by the boat.

It was now past Christmas, and the " Christmas snow " had come, whitening the ground. The Colonel's position in the chaise was one calculated to make a nervous person uneasy. The vehicle ran down on the horses' withers in the most uncomfortable way, and if the traces broke — and they had several breaks in them, mended with twine — the Colonel would be under the horses' hind feet before he knew it. But Colonel Corbin did not know what it was to be afraid of man or beast, and sat back composedly in the chaise, bracing his feet against the low dashboard, while the horses dashed along the slushy country road. The snow does not last in Eastern Virginia, and it only made the road wet and slippery to the most unsatisfactory degree. But over the fields and woods it lay soft and unsoiled. The

afternoon was gray, and a biting east wind was
blowing.

The Colonel got to the landing in ample
time, but it would be dusk before the great river
steamboat would arrive. Meanwhile, he went
into the little waiting-room, with its red-hot
stove, and conversed amicably with the wharf-
inger, a blacksmith, and two drummers, waiting to take the boat "up the bay." It was
almost dark when a long, shrill whistle resounded, and everybody jumped up, saying,
"The boat!" A truck loaded with boxes and
freight of all sorts, and the drummers' trunks,
and drawn by a patient mule, was started down
the tramway on the wharf that extended nearly
four hundred yards into the river. The Colonel, like most country gentlemen, liked to see
what was to be seen, and walked out on the
wharf to watch the exciting spectacle of the
boat making her landing.

The sky had darkened still more, and it
looked as if more snow were coming. The
great, broad salt river, with its fierce tides
and foaming like the ocean that it was so near,
was quite black, except for the phosphores-
cent glare left in the steamer's wake as she

plowed her way along, looking like a gigantic illuminated lantern with lights blazing from
one end of her to the other.   At intervals her
long, hoarse whistle screamed over the waters,
and presently, with much noise and churning,
she bumped against the wharf and was made
fast.   Her gangplank was thrown out, and a
few passengers in the humbler walks of life
stepped off; but, in a moment, the captain
himself appeared, escorting a woman in a long
fur cloak.   The light from a lantern on the
wharf fell directly upon her, and as soon as
the Colonel saw her, he understood why she
should have the captain's escort.   She was
about forty, apparently, and her abundant dark
hair was slightly streaked with gray.   But
there was not a line or a wrinkle in her clear,
pale face, and her eyes had the beauty of a
girl of fifteen.   There was something peculiarly elegant in her whole air — the long seal-
skin mantle that enveloped her, the close black
bonnet that she wore, her immaculate gloves
and shoes — Colonel Corbin at once recognized in her a metropolitan.

She remained talking with the captain for
a few moments, until he was obliged to leave.
It took only a short while to discharge the small

amount of freight, and in five minutes the boat
had lurched off, and the noise of her churning
wheels and the myriad lights from her saloons
were melting in the blackness where the river
and night sky blent together.

The stranger looked around her with calm
self-possession, and seemed surprised at the
loneliness of the landscape and the deserted
look of things around the little waiting-room
and freight-house at the end of the wharf.
Colonel Corbin, imagining her the unexpectedly arrived guest of some one in the county,
advanced with a profound bow, and taking
off his hat in the cutting blast, said :

"Madam, permit me to say that you seem
to be a stranger and to have no one to meet
you.   I am Colonel Corbin, and I should es-
teem it a privilege to be of assistance to
you."

"Thank you," she answered, turning to him
and speaking with a very French accent, "I did
not expect any one to meet me, but I thought
there would be a town — or a village at least,
when I left the steamer.   I am foreign to this
country — I am French, but I am accustomed
to traveling."

"Every word that you say, madam, is

another claim upon me. A lady, and alone in a strange country! Pray command my services. May I ask if you are a visitor to any of the county families?—for in that event everything would be very much simplified."

"Scarcely," responded the stranger, with the ghost of a smile upon her handsome face; "but I have traveled many thousand miles to have an interview with Mr. Richard Romaine. Permit me to introduce myself—I am Madame de Fonblanque."

The Colonel's face was a study as Madame de Fonblanque continued, calmly: "I should like first to go to a hotel—somewhere—and then I could arrange to meet Mr. Romaine."

"But, madam, there is no hotel, except a country tavern at the Court House, ten miles away. My residence, however, Corbin Hall, is only four miles from here—and Mr. Romaine's place, Shrewsbury, is also within that distance; and if you would accept of my hospitality, and that of my sister and my granddaughter, I should be most happy. I have here a chaise and pair, and would feel honored if you would accept of their service as well as mine."

Madame de Fonblanque then showed considerable knowledge of human nature: for

she at once agreed to trust the Colonel, although she had never laid eyes on him before.

"I think," she said, after a slight pause, "that
I shall be compelled to accept of your kindness as frankly as you offer it. I will say at
once, that as I have come to demand an act of
justice from Mr. Romaine, he may not make
any effort toward seeing me — and as he may
do me that act of justice, I must ask you to
trust me for that. But the sooner I see him
the better. If, therefore, you would drive me
at once to his château — house — I could in
a few moments discern his intentions. The
boat, I understand, passes here daily before
the sun rises — and I could leave to-morrow
morning."

The simplicity and directness of Madame de
Fonblanque's language prepossessed the Colonel still more in her favor. But at the proposition to go to Shrewsbury he winced a little.
However, there was no help for it — he had
offered to befriend her, and he stood unflinch-
ingly to his word.

"Then, madam," said the Colonel, bowing,
"it shall be my privilege to drive you to
Shrewsbury, Mr. Romaine's residence — and
from there to my own place, where my sister

and granddaughter will be happy to entertain you as long as you find it agreeable to remain with us."

"I thank you a thousand times," replied Madame de Fonblanque. "I have never met with greater kindness, and you have the gratitude of a woman and a stranger, whom you have relieved from a most inconvenient predicament."

The Colonel then offered her his arm, and together they traversed the long wharf in the descending night, while a wild east wind raved about them and made the black water seethe below them. There was not much talking in the teeth of such a wind, but when Madame de Fonblanque was seated in the chaise with the lap-robes tucked around her, and the horses were making good time along the soggy road, she told all that was necessary about herself. She was the widow of an army officer, and since her widowhood had spent much time in traveling. She had come to this country to see Mr. Romaine on a matter which she frankly declared was chiefly one of money; and she desired a personal interview with him before taking legal steps. She had had a maid with her, but the woman, having found an unexpected opportunity of going back to France, had basely left her only the day before.

"And so, as I am a soldier's daughter and a soldier's widow," she said, with a smile, "I thought, 'What can harm one in this chivalrous country? I will go alone. I will take enough money with me'—I was careful not to take too much—'and I will simply find out the quickest way to reach Mr. Romaine, and see him; and then I will return to New York, where I have friends.'"

"A very courageous thing for a lady to do, madam," replied the Colonel, gallantly. "But I think you will find, particularly in the State of Virginia, that a woman's weakness is her strength. Every Virginia gentleman is the protector of a defenseless woman."

Madame de Fonblanque smiled prettily, showing very white teeth. She did not quite understand the Colonel's allusion to Virginia gentlemen especially, but having great tact, she appeared to comprehend it perfectly.

"But do not think for a moment," she said, "that I would bestow my confidence upon all men as I have bestowed it on you. The supreme honesty of your character was perfectly visible to me the instant you addressed me.

I have seen much of the world, and I am no bad reader of character, and I trusted you from the moment I saw you."

The Colonel took off his hat, and bowed so low that the chaise, at that moment giving a lurch, nearly pitched him head foremost under his horses' heels. Madame de Fonblanque uttered a little scream.

"I always was so nervous about horses," she said; "although both my father and my husband were in the Lancers, they never could induce me to ride."

Then she began asking some questions about Mr. Romaine, which showed that she had a very clear knowledge of his character.

"And is the English mees there still?" she inquired, with a slight smile.

"Yes; but I understand that she has been desirous to leave for some time," answered the Colonel.

"Mr. Romaine is a very extraordinary man," continued Madame de Fonblanque, after a pause. "I have known him for a long time, and I do not think in all these years I have ever known him to do one thing in the usual manner."

"I have known him, madam, many more

years than you have — we were boys together
sixty years ago — and I must say your esti-
mate of him is correct.   Yet Romaine is not
without his virtues."

"Quite true," replied Madame de Fonblanque, composedly.   "He can be the most
generous of men—but I do not think he
knows what justice is."

"Precisely—precisely, madam.   After Romaine has spoiled a life, or has used the
power of his money most remorselessly, he
will then turn around and do the most generous and princely thing in the world.   But I
should not like to be in his power."

"Nor I," said Madame de Fonblanque, in
a low voice.

"At present," continued the Colonel, "the
relations between us are somewhat strained.
I am much vexed with him, and have shown
it.   But Romaine, as you say, being totally
unlike any created being, sees fit to ignore it,
and actually rides over and borrows my man
David—a worthy negro, of very inferior in-
tellect, though—to shave him!"

It did not take long to make the four miles
to Shrewsbury, and presently they dashed up
to the door of the large, brightly lighted

house, and the Colonel rapped smartly on the door. There was a bell—an innovation introduced by Mr. Romaine—but Colonel Corbin disdained to use so modern and unheard-of an appliance.

Dodson opened the door, and a flood of light from the fine old-fashioned entrance hall poured out into the night. Colonel Corbin, according to the Virginia custom, walked in, escorting Madame de Fonblanque, without asking if any one was home—somebody was certain to be at home and delighted to see visitors.

Dodson was about to usher them politely in the drawing-room, when Bridge suddenly appeared. To say that his hair stood on end when he caught sight of Madame de Fonblanque is hardly putting it strong enough. His jaw dropped, and his eyes nearly popped out of his head. He recovered himself and ran and seized the knob of the drawing-room door.

"Please," he said, in a very positive tone, "Mr. Romaine his n't at 'ome."

"How do you know that, sir?" sternly demanded the Colonel, advancing on Bridge, who still held on to the door-knob.

" Because—because—I *knows* he ain't—
to—that—'ere—pusson."

The Colonel, who was tall and strong,
caught Bridge by the coat collar, and, with
clenched teeth, shook him up and down as a
terrier shakes a rat.

" You insolent scoundrel," he said, in a
fierce basso, " I have a great mind to throw
you out of the door.   Go this instant and tell
your master that Madame de Fonblanque and
Colonel Corbin are here."

Bridge, nearly frightened out of his life,
and black in the face, was glad to escape.
He made his way half across the hall to Mr.
Romaine's study door, and then hesitated.
Afraid as he was of the Colonel, the idea of
facing Mr. Romaine with such a message was
still more terrifying.   The Colonel helped him
to make up his mind by advancing and giving
him a well-directed kick on the shins which
nearly threw him into Mr. Romaine's arms, as
that individual unexpectedly opened the door.

Then there was a pause.

Madame de Fonblanque had remained a
silent spectator of the whole scene, wearing a
look of calm amusement.   As soon as Mr.
Romaine caught sight of her, his pale face

grew still more ashy, and his inscrutable black eyes blazed with a still more somber splendor. Colonel Corbin, quite unmoved by his little rencontre with " that infernal flunkey," as he described the worthy Bridge afterward, advanced and said, with his most magnificent air :

" Allow me, Romaine, to announce a lady with whom I imagine you to have the honor of a previous acquaintance — Madame de Fonblanque."

" The devil I have!" replied Mr. Romaine.

X

COLONEL CORBIN could not kick his friend Romaine as he had done poor Bridge—but he would have dearly liked to at that moment.

Mr. Romaine, after glaring at Madame de Fonblanque, without the slightest greeting, turned to the Colonel.

"Corbin," he said, "you always were and always will be the most unsophisticated, impractical creature God ever made. The idea of your taking up with this brazen adventuress and bringing her to my house!"

"Hear me, sir," responded the Colonel; "if you utter another disparaging word respecting this lady, I will forget your age and infirmities, and give you the most genteel walloping you ever had in your life."

"It will be the first time you ever forgot my age and infirmities," coolly answered Mr.

Romaine; and then turning to Madame de Fonblanque, he said:

"What do you want of me?"

"You know very well what I want of you."

"You will never get it."

"I shall try, nevertheless. I wish to see you in private."

"Madam," said the Colonel, "if you desire the protection of my presence, you shall have it. I have not the slightest regard for this—person—who so maligned you; and you see that physically I am still worth a good deal."

"You are worth a good deal in every way," replied Madame de Fonblanque warmly. "Still, I will see Mr. Romaine alone; and when the interview is over I will again throw myself upon your protection."

Mr. Romaine turned and led the way to his library, Madame de Fonblanque following him. He closed the door, and stood waiting for her to speak. He was in the greatest rage of his life, but he did not in the least lose his self-possession.

"Well?" he said, his face blazing with the intensity of his anger.

"One hundred thousand francs," responded Madame de Fonblanque, sweetly.

They were standing in the middle of the floor, the soft light of the fire and of a great lamp on the table falling upon them.

"You have raised your price since we last met."

"Yes. I reckoned up the interest and added it. Besides, I really think a woman who was disappointed in being made your wife needs a hundred thousand francs to console her for your loss. Now, most men would not be worth more than thirty or forty thousand."

Madame de Fonblanque spoke quite cheerfully and even gaily. She tapped her pocket gracefully.

"Here I have those letters of yours. They never leave me — particularly the one proposing marriage, and the half dozen in which you call me your dearest Athanaise and reproach me bitterly for not loving you enough. Just imagine the hurricane of amusement they would cause if read out in court with proper elocutionary effect."

Madame de Fonblanque laughed, and Mr. Romaine positively blushed.

"What an infernal, infernal ass I was!"

"Yes, I thought so, too," responded the pretty and sprightly Frenchwoman — "I have

often noticed that people who can make fools
of others, invariably, at some time in their
lives, make fools of themselves."

"I did," answered Mr. Romaine, sententiously. "But I tell you, once for all, not a
penny will I pay."

"Ah, my dear M. Romaine, that is not for
you to say. These breach-of-promise cases
sometimes turn out very badly for the gentlemen. I can so easily prove my position, my
respectability—the way you pursued me from
London to Brighton, from Brighton to Folkestone, from Folkestone to Eastbourne—and
these invaluable and delightful letters. It
will be a *cause célèbre*—that you may depend
upon. And what a figure you will cut! The
New York papers will have a column a day—
the London papers two columns. By the
way, I hear you have leased a fine house at
Prince's Gate for the season. You will have
to give up that lease, my friend—you will not
dare to show your face in London this season,
M. Romaine."

All this time Madame de Fonblanque had
been laughing, as if it were a very good joke;
but she now became serious.

"There is a tragic side to it," she continued,

going closer to Mr. Romaine, and looking at
him in a threatening way. "I know all about
that visit to Dr. Chambers. No matter how
I found it out—I know he passed sentence of
death on you; and while this good, amiable
Chessingham is doctoring you for all sorts of
imaginary aches and pains, you have one constant ache and pain that he does not suspect,
because you have so carefully concealed it
from him—and the slightest annoyance or
chagrin may be fatal to you. I know that you
have tried to persuade the good Chessingham
that you have every disease in the calendar
of diseases—except the one that is killing
you."

Mr. Romaine walked rather unsteadily to a
chair and sat down, burying his face in his
hands. Madame de Fonblanque, after a moment, felt an impulse of pity toward him. She
went and touched him lightly.

"You called me a brazen adventuress just
now—and I acknowledge that I am not engaged in a very high business, trying to make
you pay me for not keeping your word. But
I feel sorry for you now. I dislike to witness
your unhappiness. Say you will pay me, and
let me go."

"Never," answered Mr. Romaine, looking up, with an unquenchable determination in his eyes.

"Very well, then," answered Madame de Fonblanque, quietly; "you know I am a very determined woman. I came here to see for myself what your condition is. I shall go away to instruct my lawyers to bring suit against you immediately. I may not get one hundred thousand francs in money—but I will get a hundred thousand francs' worth of revenge."

"It seems to me," presently said Mr. Romaine, with a cynical smile on his face, "your revenge will be two-edged."

"So is nearly all revenge. It's a very ignoble thing to avenge one's self—few people can do it without sharing in the ignominy. But I weighed the matter well before I made up my mind. French newspapers take but little notice of what goes on outside of Paris. I have influence enough to silence those that would say anything about it—and I care not a sou for anybody or anything in this country or England. I shall go back to Paris and say it was another Madame de Fonblanque."

Madame de Fonblanque, following Mr. Romaine's example, seated herself, and opened the long, rich cloak of fur she wore. She was certainly very handsome, particularly when the heat of the room brought a slight flush to her clear cheeks.

"It is strange to me that a woman of your education and standing should engage in this scheme of yours," after a while said Mr. Romaine.

"One hundred thousand francs," responded Madame de Fonblanque.

"You might have married well a dozen times if you had played your cards right," he continued.

"One hundred thousand francs," again said Madame de Fonblanque.

"What are your plans of campaign, may I ask?"

"To get one hundred thousand francs from you."

"That ridiculous old blunderbuss, Corbin! I suppose he has invited you to take up your quarters at Corbin Hall, indefinitely, without knowing any more about you than he does of the man in the moon."

"He has — the dear, innocent old gentle-man — and I shall stay until I get my one

hundred thousand francs. But he shall not
regret it. I know how to appreciate kindness. I have met with so little. The man I
loved — my husband — squandered my *dot*,
which I gave him, and it is on account of my
rash fondness for one man that it is now absolutely necessary for me to have some money
from another; and I intend to make every
effort to get a hundred thousand francs from
you."

Mr. Romaine remained silent for a few
minutes, considering a *coup*. Then his usual
sly smile appeared upon his countenance.
When he spoke his voice had more than its
usual velvety softness.

"Your efforts, Madame de Fonblanque,
will not be necessary; for I hereby declare to
you my perfect willingness to marry you, and
I shall put it in writing."

It was now Madame de Fonblanque's turn
to be disconcerted. She fell back in her chair
and gazed dumbly at Mr. Romaine. Marry
him! And as she had laughed while Mr.
Romaine had suffered, now he laughed wickedly while she literally cowered at the prospect presented to her.

"And as regards my sudden and speedy

death, which you seem to anticipate, it could not benefit you " — he leaned over and said something to her in a low tone, which caused Madame de Fonblanque to start — "so that you will have the satisfaction of enjoying my money — such as I may choose to give you — as long as I live. But I warn you — I am not an easy man to live with, nor would the circumstances of our marriage render me more so. Ask Chessingham if I am easy to live with, and he will tell you that I am not, even at my best. It would not surprise me, in case our marriage took place, if you were to wish yourself free again. You say you desire revenge. So would I — and I would take it."

Madame de Fonblanque grew steadily paler as Mr. Romaine spoke. She knew well enough the purgatory he was offering her. To marry him! Such an idea had never dawned upon her. The conviction of his insincerity had caused her coyness in the first instance which had stimulated Mr. Romaine so much. It had really looked, in the beginning, as if he would not succeed in the least in making a fool of this pretty French widow. But he had finally succeeded at the cost of making a fool of himself. However, it was

now his turn to score — because it was plain
that Madame de Fonblanque was anything
but enraptured at the notion of marrying him.

She caught sight of Mr. Romaine's black
eyes dancing in enjoyment of her predicament.
She rose and drew her fur cloak around her.

"I will think it over, Mr. Romaine," she
said, calmly.

"Pray do," responded Mr. Romaine; "and
I will write you a letter to-morrow morning,
making a specific offer to fulfil my promise,
which will make those cherished letters of
yours worth considerably less than the paper
they are written on — and what a honeymoon
we will have!"

At this, Madame de Fonblanque positively
shuddered, but she held her head up bravely
as Mr. Romaine opened the door politely for
her, and they discovered Colonel Corbin
stalking up and down the hall alone.

"Corbin," said Mr. Romaine, blandly,
"Madame de Fonblanque and I have reached
a perfectly satisfactory agreement."

"Sir," replied the Colonel, glowering with
wrath, "it must also be made satisfactory to
me. When I bring a lady to a house, she is
under my protection; and when she has the

term 'brazen adventuress' applied to her,
simply because she has come to demand a
mere act of justice — and I know this to be a
fact, because she has so informed me — I must
insist upon an apology from the person apply-
ing that term."

"Very well, then," said Mr. Romaine, debo-
nair and smiling. "I apologize. Madame de
Fonblanque is not a brazen adventuress — she
is merely a lady of great enterprise and assurance, and I wish you joy of her acquaintance."

In Madame de Fonblanque's breast there
sprang up that desire that is never wholly
smothered in any human being — to appear
well in the presence of a person she respected.
She did sincerely respect Colonel Corbin, who
had befriended her on that risky expedition,
and it cut her to the heart to be insulted before him. Her eyes filled with tears, and she
turned to him with trembling lips.

"Do not mind what he says. He hates me
because he has injured me, and keeps me out
of money that he ought to pay me."

"I do not mind him in the least, madam,"
replied the Colonel, suavely. "Mr. Romaine
knows perfectly well my opinion of him. He

keeps you out of money he owes you, and in-
sists upon forcing on my granddaughter money
that she does not want, and which will involve
her in endless trouble.   I think that is quite
characteristic of Romaine.   Let us now leave
this inhospitable house."

Madame de Fonblanque took the arm the
Colonel offered her, and walked out of the
hall without noticing Mr. Romaine's courteous
bow.

The proposition made to Madame de Fonblanque was truly startling. Almost anything
on earth was better than marrying him — and
what he had whispered to her proved that she
could not profit one penny by his death.   She
would gladly have foregone that offer on paper
for some other letters she had in which he flatly
refused to keep his word, and which she had
held over him *in terrorem*.   She could not de-
termine in a moment what to do, but she was
convinced that she could not see Mr. Romaine
again, and the matter would have to be settled
by correspondence.   And then she felt the
sooner she got away from this place where she
had been checkmated the better.   When they
were traveling fast through the murky night
toward Corbin Hall, she broached the subject

at once of her return in the morning. The
Colonel declared it depended upon the weather,
which puzzled Madame de Fonblanque very
much until it was explained to her that it was a
question of weather whether the boat came or
not. Sometimes, in that climate, the river froze
over, and then the river steamers stopped running until there was a thaw—for ice-boats
were unknown in that region. It was very
cold, and getting colder, and the Colonel was
of the opinion that a freeze was upon them,
and no boat could get down the river that
night.

When they got to Corbin Hall, Madame de
Fonblanque was extremely nervous about the
greeting she would get from the Colonel's
womenkind—but it was as cordial and unsuspicious as his had been. The Colonel explained that Madame de Fonblanque had business with Mr. Romaine, who had treated her
like—Mr. Romaine; and Letty, as soon as
she found somebody with a community of prejudice against the master of Shrewsbury, felt
much drawn toward her. There was no doubt
that Madame de Fonblanque was a lady; and
in the innocent and unworldly lives of the ladies
at Corbin Hall, the desperate shifts and devices

to get money of people with adventurous
tendencies were altogether unknown and un-
suspected. Besides, people from a foreign
country were very great novelties to them;
and Letty seated herself, after tea, to hear all
about that marvelous world beyond the sea.
The Colonel still talked about his visit to Europe in 1835, and Paris in the days of the Cit-
izen King, and imagined that everything had
remained unchanged since then. Madame
de Fonblanque was a stout Monarchist, as
most French people of dubious antecedents
profess to be, and gave out with much tact
that, although only the widow of a poor
officer in the Lancers, she was on intimate
terms with all the Faubourg St. Germains.
As she frankly admitted her modest means,
there was no hint of braggadocio in anything
she said in her fluent French-English. She
had great curiosity about Mr. Romaine, and
was well up in all his adventures since he had
been in America. She spoke of him so coolly
and critically that it never dawned upon her
listeners that the difficulties between them
were not of the usual business kind.

"As for the English mees," she said, calmly,
"I would say to her, 'Go home, my pretty

demoiselle; don't waste your time on that—
that aged crocodile.' The English, you know,
have no sentiment. They call us unfeeling
because French parents select a suitable man
for an innocent young daughter to marry, and
bid her feel for him all the tenderness possible. But those calculating English meeses
would marry old Scaramouch himself if he
had money enough."

The Colonel did not like to hear his favor-
ite nation abused, and rather squirmed under
this; but he reflected that Madame de Fonblanque's remarks were due, no doubt, to the
traditional jealousy between the French and
the English.

Madame de Fonblanque gave the straight-
est possible account of herself, including the
desertion of her maid the day before.

" I thought, with my trusty Suzanne, I could
face anything. I did not imagine I could go
anywhere in this part of America that I would
not find hotels, railroads, telegraph offices —"

" There is one tavern in the county, and
that a very poor one, six miles away — and not
a line of telegraph wire or railway nearer than
two counties off," explained Letty, smiling.

Madame de Fonblanque clapped her hands.

"How delicious! I shall tell this in France. It is like some of our retired places in the provinces, where the government has erected telegraph lines, but the people do not know exactly what they are meant for! And when that wretched Suzanne left me, I asked at once for the French consul — but I found there was none in town. All of my adventures here have been novel — and as I have met with such very great kindness, I shall always regard them as amusing."

She showed no disposition to trespass on the hospitality so generously offered her, and looked out of the window anxiously when they rose to go to their rooms. But it had begun snowing early in the evening, and the ground was now perfectly white.

"No boat to-morrow, madam," said the Colonel. "You will, I am sure, be forced to content yourself at Corbin Hall for some days yet."

"I content myself perfectly," replied Madame de Fonblanque, with ready grace; "but one must be careful not to take advantage of so much generosity as yours."

When she was alone in the same old-fashioned bedroom that Farebrother had occupied, enjoying, as he had done, the sparkling wood fire, she reflected gratefully upon the goodness of these refined and simple-minded people — but she also reflected with much bitterness upon the extremely slim prospect of her getting any money from Mr. Romaine. She had fully counted upon his dread of ridicule, his fear of publicity, to induce him to hand over a considerable sum of money; but she had not in the least counted upon what she considered his truly diabolical offer to come up to his word. To marry Mr. Romaine! She could have brought herself to it, reflecting that he could not live forever; but those few words he whispered to her showed her that it was out of her power to get any money at his death. She believed what he told her — it was so thoroughly characteristic of him — and she would by no means risk the horrors of marrying this embodied whim with that probability hanging over her. She turned it over and over in her mind, wearily, until past midnight, when she tossed to and fro until the gray dawn shone upon the snow-covered world.

But Mr. Romaine suffered from more than sleeplessness that night. The Chessinghams guessed from the accounts given by the ser-

vants of the strange visitor that Madame de
Fonblanque had turned up miraculously with
Colonel Corbin, and after a short interview with
Mr. Romaine had disappeared. They knew
all about the old report that Mr. Romaine had
been very marked in his attentions at one time
to the pretty widow, and Chessingham shrewdly guessed very near the truth concerning her
visit, which truth convulsed him with laughter.

"It is the most absurd thing," he said to his
wife and Ethel Maywood, in their own sitting
room that night. "No doubt the old fellow
has some entanglement with her, and finding
widows a little more difficult to impose upon
than guileless maidens, he's been trapped in
some way."

"And serves him right," said Mrs. Chessingham, with energy. "I know he's kind to
us, Reggie — but — was there ever such another man as Mr. Romaine, do you think?"

"The Lord be praised, no," answered
Chessingham. "And he is not only mentally
and morally different from any man I ever
saw, but physically, too. I swear, after having
been his doctor for two years, I don't know
his constitution yet. He will describe to me
the most contradictory symptoms. He will

profess to take a prescription and apparently
it will have just the opposite effect from that
intended. Sometimes I have asked myself if
he has not, all the time, some disease that he
rigorously conceals from me, and he simply
uses these subterfuges to deceive me."

"Anything is possible with Mr. Romaine,"
said Ethel quietly. "And yet — he is the
most generous of men. Our own father was
not half so free with his money to us as Mr.
Romaine is. And he seems to shrink from
the least acknowledgment of it. How many
men, do you think, would allow a doctor to
carry his wife and sister-in-law around with
him as he does, and do everything for us, as if
we were the most valued friends and guests?"

"Oh, Romaine isn't a bad man, so much as
a perverse one," replied Chessingham, lightly,
"and he is a tremendously interesting one."

At that very moment, Mr. Romaine was in
the condition that any man but himself would
have called for a doctor — but not for worlds
would he have allowed Chessingham to see
him then. He understood his own case perfectly — and the one human being near him
that was in his confidence was Bridge.

The evening was a very unhappy one for

Mr. Romaine — the more so that what the great specialist he had consulted had predicted was actually happening. Being disturbed in mind, he was becoming ill in body. How on earth had that cruel French woman found out about Dr. Chambers? So Mr. Romaine thought, sitting in his library chair, suffering acutely. Dr. Chessingham offered to come in and read to him, to play écarté with him — but it occurred to Mr. Romaine that perhaps a visit to the Chessinghams' part of the house might divert his spirits and take his mind off the torturing subject of Madame de Fonblanque. He took Bridge's arm and tottered off to the Chessinghams' sitting-room. But the instant he entered the door his indomitable spirit asserted itself. He stood upright, walked steadily, and even forced a smile to his lips. Mrs. Chessingham and Ethel were at their everlasting fancy work, of which Mr. Romaine had never seen a completed specimen. Ethel rose and placed a chair for him — which, as he was old and infirm and needed it, nettled him extremely.

"Pray, my dear Miss Maywood, don't trouble yourself. I do not yet require the kind coddling you would bestow upon me."

Ethel, being an amiable and patient creature, took this with a smile.

"I am looking forward with great pleasure," said Mr. Romaine, after having seated
himself in a straight-backed chair, while he
yearned for an easy one, "to the season in
London. I have had my eye on that house
in Prince's Gate for several years, and, of
course, feel pleased to have it. Being an old-
fashioned man, I have kept pretty closely to
the localities which were modish when I was
a young attaché some years since — such as
Belgravia, Grosvenor, and Lowndes Squares,
and all those places. But there is something very attractive about the new Ken-
sington — and I have intended for some years
to take a house in that part of town for a
season — and this one particularly struck my
fancy."

"It is very handsome — but very expensive," said Mrs. Chessingham.

"Most handsome things are expensive, dear
madam, but this house is reasonable, considering its charm, and I hope that you as well as
your sister will enjoy some of its pleasures
with me."

Both young women smiled — it would be

nice to have the run of the house at Prince's
Gate — and after going through with a winter in the country, and in Virginia, too, they
thought they had earned it.

"Heretofore," continued Mr. Romaine,
stroking his white mustache with his delicate
hand, "while I have been fond of entertaining,
it has always been of a sedate kind — chiefly
dinners. But last year I was beguiled into
promising my young friend, Lady Gwendolen
Beauclerc, a ball, if I could get a house with
a ball-room — and a few days ago I received
a very pretty reminder of my promise, in the
shape of a photograph and a letter."

"Better and better," thought Ethel — "to be
invited to a ball given to please Lady Gwendolen Beauclerc!" But Gladys spoke up with
her usual simplicity and straightforwardness.

"I hardly think, being now married to a
medical man with his way to make in the
world, that I shall be asked to many swell
balls—and perhaps it is better that I should
not go."

"But, Gladys, we went once to swell balls,"
said Ethel, reproachfully.

"Oh, yes," answered Gladys, "but that
was over and done with when I married my

husband — and he is well worth the sacrifice. Reggie himself is of good family, as you know, but he is on that account too proud to associate with people upon terms of condescension — so, when we were married, we agreed to be very careful about giving and accepting invitations."

"The social prejudices of you English are peculiar," remarked Mr. Romaine. "It is from you that we Virginia people inherit that profound respect for land. I found, early in life, when I first went to England and when Americans were scarce there, that it was more in my favor to be a landholder and a slave-owner than if I had been worth millions. The landed people in all countries are united by a powerful bond, which does not seem to exist with other forms of property. But because agriculture is perhaps the first and the most absorbing and conservative of all industrial callings, the people who own land are naturally bound together and appreciative of each other."

While Mr. Romaine was giving this little disquisition, he suffered furious pain, but the only indication he gave of it was a furtive wiping of his brow.

"And the hold of the land upon one is peculiar. I could never bring myself to part with an acre of it which I had either bought or inherited. Of course, during my practical expatriation for many years, my landed property here has suffered. I have often wondered at myself for holding on to it, when I could have invested the money in an English estate which really would have been much more profitable — but I could never divest myself of the feeling that the land would yet draw me back to it. However," he continued, quite gaily, " it is now so depreciated, and the new system is so impossible for the old masters to adopt, that I can't sell it, and I can't live on it — so I shall be compelled to buy an estate in England in the country, for a town house, even the Prince's Gate one, is only endurable for five months in the year."

Ethel's eyes glistened — a town house at Prince's Gate — an estate in the country! Might she not, after all, be Mrs. Romaine? And Mr. Romaine's position was so much better than that of any other American she knew ; the others were all striving for recognition, but Mr. Romaine had had an assured place in English society for a generation. He

had not only dandled Lady Gwendolen Beauclerc, who was a duke's daughter, on his knee,
but he had danced, at a court ball, with the
Queen herself, when she was a youthful matron,
and he was a slim young diplomat.   And in a
flash of imagination, Ethel saw herself be-
comingly attired in widow's weeds and leaving, by the hands of a footman in mourning
livery, black-bordered cards, bearing the in-
scription, " *Mrs. Romaine.*"

XI

AT last, Mr. Romaine was conquered by pain, and rose to leave the Chessinghams' rooms about ten o'clock. As he said good-night, some strange impulse made him take Ethel's soft, white hand in his, which was deathly cold and clammy. He looked at her in her fresh, wholesome beauty. He knew she was just as designing in her own way as Madame de Fonblanque — but the designing was different in the two women, according to their race. Ethel's was the peculiarly artless and primitive designing, which is as near as the English character can come to deception — for it really deceives nobody. Madame de Fonblanque's was the consummate designing of the Latin races, which could deceive almost anybody. At that very moment she was completely hoodwinking the people at Corbin Hall, and Letty, who had been disgusted with Ethel's transparent devices to ensnare Mr. Romaine, never for a moment suspected that the graceful and tactful Madame de Fonblanque's " business " with Mr. Romaine was an attempt to entrap him of a nature much more desperate and barefaced than Ethel would have dreamed of.

But as Mr. Romaine looked into Ethel's rosy, fresh face, he saw a great deal of good there. She would not bedevil him as the French woman had done. She was amiable even in her disappointments, and if things had been otherwise, and she could have shared with him the town house, and the country house, and the carriage, would have tended him faithfully and kindly. Some dim idea of rewarding her by making her an offer as soon as he was clear of the French woman dawned upon his mind. Ethel, for her part, read a new look of gentleness in his expressive black eyes — and his hand-clasp was positively tender. But his pain showed in his glance — there was something agonizing in his eyes as Ethel's met his. And fascinated by them she gazed into them with a strange and pathetic feeling that it was not " good-night " she was saying, but " good-by." Mr. Romaine himself had something of this feeling

—and so for a full minute they stood hand in hand, and quite silent. Mrs. Chessingham moved away judiciously — and did not return until the door closed behind Mr. Romaine. Ethel stood in the same spot, with a pained face.

"Do you know, Gladys, I had a queer feeling just now — as if Mr. Romaine were really ill, and might die at any time? And all the time we have looked upon him as a hypochondriac."

"Reggie says if anybody really expected Mr. Romaine to die he would live forever. But I have not heard him say he was ill, and I am sure Reggie does not suspect it. And, Ethel dear, I should n't be surprised if, after all, that house at Prince's Gate should be yours."

"*I* should be," answered Ethel, "but if it ever is, I promise to be kind to the old gentleman."

Bridge had met "the old gentleman" just outside the door, and had gone with him to the library, where he sat within easy call. Mr. Romaine, seated at his table, after a while seemed to recover from his paroxysm of pain. He unlocked a drawer and took out his will, which he read over, smiling all the time — he

seemed to regard it as a very facetious document. Then he added something to it. He
had a few valuable diamonds which he had
collected for no particular purpose some years
before, and he thought that Ethel Maywood
might as well have them. And then he wrote
his offer to Madame de Fonblanque, and sealed
and addressed it. It seemed to give him
such acute pleasure that he almost forgot his
pain. He smiled, his black eyes sparkled,
he smoothed his mustache coquettishly, and
thought to himself:

" Checkmated, by Jove ! "

It was then near twelve o'clock, and he rang
for Bridge and went to his bedroom.

The man undressed him and put him to bed,
and then Mr. Romaine said casually :

" You had better sit in this room to-night."

Even with this servant, who knew the whole
secret of his ailments, Mr. Romaine maintained a systematic kind of deceit which did
not deceive.

Bridge stirred the fire into a ruddy blaze,
and sat down by it to doze. Occasionally he
rose and went toward the luxurious bed, where
Mr. Romaine lay with wide-open, staring eyes,
and every few moments he wanted something

done for him. This alarmed Bridge, but he dared not show his uneasiness. At last, about two o'clock in the morning, when he had given up all attempts at dozing, he heard a sound which made him jump. It was a slight groan.

In all the sixteen years that he had served Mr. Romaine he had never known from him the slightest sign that pain was victor. Bridge fairly ran to the bed at this.

"What's the matter?" sternly asked Mr. Romaine.

"Did n't I hear you groan, sir?"

"Of course not — Bridge, you are in your dotage."

Bridge went back to his place. In ten minutes came another groan — and another.

He rose and went to the bedside again.

"Mr. Romaine, I 'm a-goin' for Mr. Chessingham. I can't stand this no longer."

"I should think if I could stand it, you could."

"No, sir. Can't nobody stand what you can stand, and I 'm a-goin' for Mr. Chessingham."

"If you dare," said Mr. Romaine.

Bridge moved toward the door. By a tremendous effort Mr. Romaine rose up in bed, and seizing a carafe of water from the table at his side, sent it whizzing after Bridge. It missed its target by a very close shave, indeed.

" Next time," said Mr. Romaine, " I will aim better."

Bridge returned to his seat by the fire.

All night the struggle went on. Mr. Romaine writhed in agony, but the determination to disappoint Bridge brought him out alive. When morning broke, the worst was over, and he seemed as likely to live as he had done at any time since Bridge first knew him. But the unhappy valet showed the terrible experience he had been through with, and his pallid face and nervous hands brought a grim smile to Mr. Romaine's face.

About ten o'clock Mr. Romaine announced that he would rise and dress, having made, many years before, a secret resolution that he would die with his boots on. Bridge, completely subdued, assisted at this toilet, and helped him into the library.

While shaving him, though, Mr. Romaine said, crossly :

" You are so afraid I am dying that you 'll probably cut my throat out of pure nervousness. I have half a mind to send for that black barber at Corbin Hall, who can give you points on shaving."

Bridge was so frightened and uneasy about Mr. Romaine's condition that he did not even resent this slur.

It was still intensely cold and snowing. But the roaring fire and heavy curtains made the room deliciously comfortable. Chessingham always came to Mr. Romaine at eleven — and on this particular morning he found Mr. Romaine in his usual place before the great, cheery fireplace. But he undoubtedly looked ill.

"What sort of a night did you have?" was the young doctor's first inquiry.

"Only fairly good," replied Mr. Romaine, and then went on with great seriousness to describe a multitude of trifling symptoms, such as any imaginative person can conjure up at any moment.

"The fact is,— to be perfectly candid with you,"— said Chessingham, who was a conscientious man, "if you allow yourself to dwell upon these trifling ailments they will entail real suffering upon you. Try and forget about your stiff shoulder, and your neuralgic headache, and that sort of thing."

"But my dear fellow," answered Mr. Romaine, with a flash of humor in his black eyes, "you know it is my infirmity to exaggerate my aches and pains. Last night, for what I acknowledge was a mere trifle, I actually lay in my bed and groaned." This was for Bridge's benefit, who was putting on Mr. Romaine's immaculate boots at that moment.

Chessingham, however, did not know exactly what to make of Mr. Romaine's statement. His practised eye saw that something was the matter. But if Mr. Romaine refused to tell the doctor whom he hired to take care of his health what ailed him, the doctor was not to blame. Chessingham went back to his part of the house, much puzzled and deeply annoyed.

"Do you know," he said to his wife, "I doubt very much if I did a wise thing in accepting Mr. Romaine's offer to stay with him. My object, of saving enough from my salary to start me in London, will be attained. But suppose Mr. Romaine should die of some disease that he has concealed from me — my professional reputation would be hurt."

Gladys said some comforting words, and told him about Mr. Romaine's plans for buying an estate in England, the Prince's Gate house, the impending ball, etc. At every word she said, Chessingham looked more and more gloomy.

"Very bad, very bad," he said. "Worse and worse. He must be very ill, indeed, if he thinks it necessary to talk that way."

Gladys laughed at Chessingham's interpretation of Mr. Romaine's remarks, and reminded him of his oft-repeated prediction that Mr. Romaine would live to bury all of them.

"It is simply the same old puzzle," he said at last, impatiently. "I thought heretofore that nothing ailed him except his diabolically ingenious imagination. Now, I believe that everything ails him — but I cannot tell."

The day passed on with leaden feet to Mr. Romaine, sitting, suffering and smiling, in his easy chair. At six o'clock, he called for Bridge to dress him for the evening as usual. Bridge, thoroughly frightened, turned pale at this.

"Mr. Romaine," he said, pleadingly, "I'm afraid, sir, it'll — be the death of you."

"You'll be the death of me another way," vigorously responded Mr. Romaine. "You'll enrage me so that I'll break a blood vessel."

Bridge went and got the necessary things,

and Mr. Romaine made a ghastly toilet. He
was always particular about the tying of his
white cravat, and on this especial evening almost took poor Bridge's head off and ruined
four ties before one was done to suit him. When
he got through, he was gasping for breath,
but perfectly undaunted.

The nervous apprehension of the young
doctor about Mr. Romaine communicated itself
to everybody at Shrewsbury. They all, from
the Chessinghams and Miss Maywood down
to the very house dogs, that whined in their
loneliness and imprisonment to the house, felt
as if something ghastly and terrible was descending with the night. All except Mr. Romaine himself, who maintained an uncanny
sort of gaiety all day long, and who, every
time Chessingham visited him, was found
cackling over some humorous journals that
had arrived a day or two before. But the
young doctor could not quite appreciate the
funny cartoons and lively jokes, and his grave
face seemed to afford Mr. Romaine much sat-
urnine amusement.

The day that was so long at Shrewsbury
was very short at Corbin Hall. The Colonel
was simply delighted with Madame de Fon-

blanque, and harangued to Letty privately
upon Romaine's deuced unchivalric conduct
to a noble, attractive, and blameless woman.
This excellent man had accepted Madame de
Fonblanque at her face value.   Letty was
more worldly wise than the Colonel, but
she, too, had fallen a victim to Madame de
Fonblanque's charms and was only too ready
to think Mr. Romaine a brute.

After a delightful day, spent chiefly in the
comfortable old library, where they could bid
defiance to the cold and snow without, a
wholly unexpected visitor turned up just at
nightfall.   A loud knock at the front door,
much yelping of dogs and stamping of booted
feet announced an arrival.

There had been an understanding that Sir
Archy was to repeat his visit later in the
winter.   He was liable to arrive at any day,
and when the commotion in the large and
dusky hall was heard, the Colonel only voiced
the general impression of the group around
the library fire when he said:

" It is no doubt our kinsman, Sir Archibald."
But it was not " Sir Archibald " — and the
next minute Farebrother came walking in, as
if he had just been around the corner.   His

face was ruddy with the biting wintry air, and his eyes were bright.

The Colonel was openly charmed to see him; so was Miss Jemima, and Letty's face turned such a rosy red that it told a little story of its own. Farebrother explained that he was on his way home from the South on a professional trip, and had written that he would stop over two or three days at Corbin Hall. His letters had not been received — the mails being conducted upon a happy-go-lucky schedule in that part of the world — and on finding the river closed by ice when he left the railway twenty-five miles away, he had hired horses and had driven the distance that day in spite of the storm.

It was certainly good to see him — he was so cheerful, so manly, so full of fresh and breezy life. When he, as it were, was dragged into the library by the Colonel, Madame de Fonblanque was not present — she had gone to her room for a little rest before supper. In a little while the Colonel began to tell about her — and once started on a theme, he could not resist airing his opinion of "Romaine's utter want of courtesy and consideration for a woman."

Farebrother's countenance was a study
during all this. When the Colonel had left
the room, he turned to Letty and said, half
laughing as he spoke, " Is it possible that
Colonel Corbin picked up Madame de Fonblanque at the river landing and brought her
here to stay until she chooses to quit ? "

" Of course," answered Letty, tartly. "What
else was there left to do ? "

A great part of Farebrother's enjoyment
of his Corbin Hall friends consisted in their
simplicity and the number of hearty laughs
they afforded him.

" I declare, Miss Corbin," he exclaimed,
after indulging himself in a masculine ha-ha,
" it 's a great thing to know a place where one
can get a new sensation. It can always be
had in Virginia. You are certainly the sim-
plest people about some things and the
shrewdest about others I ever saw."

"Thank you," answered Letty, smiling, "but,
please, as I am not quite a woman of the world
yet — tell me what is the matter with Madame
de Fonblanque ? "

" Nothing on earth that I know of. But
there is room for suspicion in everybody's
mind who knows the world. What is her

mysterious business with Mr. Romaine? Likely
as not, blackmail."

Letty jumped as Farebrother said this; for
at that moment the door opened and Madame
de Fonblanque entered.

Within ten minutes after her introduction to
Farebrother, Letty saw a subtile change in her.
She exchanged her charming candor and
frank personal conversation for the guarded
manner of a woman who knows a good deal
about this wicked world, and she conversed upon
the safest and most general subjects. When
the Colonel returned they all went in to supper,
which boasted seven different kinds of bread,
served by Dad Davy with his grandest flour-
ishes. But the Colonel's delightful assumption
that Madame de Fonblanque would be their
guest for at least a month, and would probably
return in the autumn, "when the climate of
old Virginia, madam, is truly glorious and life-
giving," did not meet with the same enthusi-
astic acceptance from Madame de Fonblanque
as it had done at dinner.

The truth was, with Farebrother's keen eyes
upon her, and his polite but guarded manner
toward her, she was dealing with a different
person from the innocent old Colonel and the

unsuspicious Letty. The conversation turned
upon Mr. Romaine. The Colonel glowered
darkly, and growled below his breath that
Romaine, with age and eccentricities, was becoming intolerable. Madame de Fonblanque
shrugged her shoulders.

"I hope none of you will be so unhappy as to
have business transactions with Mr. Romaine.
You will certainly find him a very difficult
person." She said Farebrother seemed to
be the only friend that Mr. Romaine had at
the table.

"There's really a great deal that is engag-
ing and even admirable about him," he said.
"He is a man of great natural astuteness, and
if he took a stand he would be apt to know
his ground well, so that he could hold it."

Madame de Fonblanque flashed a look at
Farebrother, which he met with a cool smile.
She knew that he suspected her, and he knew
that she knew he suspected her. Her sur-
roundings were entirely novel to her; her
hosts were like the old provincial gentry in
the remote corners of France, and such people
are always much alike, and easy to hoodwink.
She was grateful to them for their kindness,
and had no thought of deceiving them any

more than was necessary. But Farebrother was a type of man that she knew all about; well learned in the ways of the world, superlatively honest, but fully able to protect himself against scamps of either sex. She wondered if he had not heard some talk about the affair between Mr. Romaine and herself — and at that very moment, she was almost overcome by chagrin and disappointment. She was desperately in need of money, despite her fur cloak and her expensive finery, and she had felt from the moment Mr. Romaine spoke that there was not the slightest chance of her getting any money from him. She wanted to write to England and consult her lawyer there before taking any further steps, and it had occurred to her, as the most convenient arrangement, to await his reply at Corbin Hall. And besides, what a rage it would put Mr. Romaine in ! But if this robust and slightly bold person, with his cheerful manner and his alert blue eyes, were to be there, Madame de Fonblanque would rather be somewhere else.

The Colonel was much puzzled because Madame de Fonblanque and Farebrother were not hail-fellow-well-met, and felt very much as if Farebrother were guilty of a want

of chivalry — but still, there was nothing to
take hold of, for he was perfectly courteous to
her.   But she had nothing more to say about
her intimacy with the old royalist families, and
when Farebrother boldly avowed himself a
firm believer in the French republic, Madame
de Fonblanque did not sigh and say, "Ah, if
you had ancestors who died for Louis and
Charles and Louis Philippe, you would not
love the republic," as she had done when
Letty advanced the same view.   In short,
Madame de Fonblanque had met her match.

As soon as supper was over she excused
herself and went to her room for an hour or
two.   She really felt depressed and unequal
to keeping up the strain any longer at that
time.   The Colonel tramped down to the
stable in the snow, to see that Tom Battercake had made the horses comfortable for the
night; and Miss Jemima always remained an
hour in the dining room after every meal, in
close confabulation with the cook.   Letty and
Farebrother went alone to the library.

The lamps were lighted, but the fire needed
a vigorous poking, which Letty proceeded to
administer, going down on her knees.   Farebrother, who knew better than to interfere,

stood by the hearth watching her. When she had got through, he suddenly went up close to her and caught her hands in his.

" Letty," he said, in a firm and serious voice that she had never heard him use before, " do you know what I came here for ? "

In an instant she knew. But the knowledge staggered her. The idea that Farebrother would take the bit between his teeth and break through all her maze of little coquetries like that had never dawned upon her. In another minute he had made his meaning so plain to her that there was no evading it.

For the first time Farebrother saw a frightened look come into her clear eyes. She turned pale, but she made no effort to escape from him. He told her that he loved her well, with the manly force and directness that women like, and Letty stammered some sweet, incoherent answer which revealed that she too knew the exaltation of life's great fever. All her pretty airs and graces dropped from her in a moment—she stood trembling, and unconsciously returned the clasp of Farebrother's strong hands, like some weak creature holding desperately to one that is all steadfastness. Farebrother could not recall afterward one word that he had said; he only remembered that he felt as if they two stood alone on some cloud-capped peak, the whole world vanished from their sight, but sunshine above them and all around them.

Two tears dropped from Letty's eyes, she knew not why, and Farebrother consoled her, for what he did not know—and they drank the wine of life together. But after a while they came from their own heaven down to a real world that was scarcely less beautiful to them.

Almost the first rational question Farebrother asked her was—"And how about that good-looking villain of an Englishman?"

"My cousin Archibald? Why, he never asked me to be Lady Corbin."

"Thank the Lord." There was a good deal more sincerity in this thanksgiving than might have been suspected.

"Do you think I would have been dazzled by his title and money?" asked Letty, offended.

"No, because you don't know anything about either money or titles. You are a very clever girl, my dear, but you are very unsophisticated, so far. I believe, though, he

would have to come down here among you
quaint Virginia people to find any girl who
would n't take him.   And the sinner is a
deuced fine fellow—that I must admit."

"I *did* want the honor and glory of refusing him," Letty admitted, candidly, "but he
never gave me the chance, more 's the pity."

Farebrother burst into a ringing laugh.
Letty's ideas on the subject of love and court-
ship had a unique and childish candor which
delighted a man who knew as much about
this ridiculous old planet as Farebrother.

Their love making was cut short by the
Colonel's and Miss Jemima's entrance.   Colonel Corbin at once engaged Farebrother in
a red-hot political discussion.   The Colonel
was a believer in states' rights to the point of
not believing in a central government at all,
and Letty ably assisted him by ready refer-
ences to the Constitution of the United States.
But Farebrother was a match for them both,
and argued that Washington, Hamilton, and a
great many of the fathers wanted a central
government a great deal stronger than their
successors of to-day are prepared to accept.
The Colonel, though, was rather disgusted to
observe that Letty and Farebrother were half

laughing while they argued and quarrelled, and that Letty wore a very sweet smile when once or twice the Colonel was unhorsed in the discussion. From politics they fell into talk about Mr. Romaine, and in the midst of it a tap came at the door, and Madame de Fonblanque entered.

"We were again discussing our eccentric friend Romaine, Madame," said the Colonel, anxious lest Madame de Fonblanque should suppose that her arrival was an interruption. "Mr. Farebrother seems to take a more indulgent view of him than any of us do."

"For my part," answered Madame de Fonblanque, with a gesture of aversion, "I do not hesitate to say that I dislike Mr. Romaine very much. I cannot deny that he is a gentleman—"

"Technically, my dear madam—technically—"

"— But I believe, if he were to die tomorrow, he would not leave behind him one heart to ache for him."

Just then the door opened, and Dad Davy presented a solemn, scared face.

"Marse Colonel," he said, "dee done sont dat white man, Dodson, f'um Shrewsbury, an'

he say Mr. Romaine mighty sick an' dee 'feerd
he gwine die, and he want Madame Fire-
block — or whatever she name — ter come
right away. Dee got a kerridge and hosses
out d'yar and de white man k'yarn leave 'em."

A sudden chill and silence fell upon them
all at this. Mr. Romaine must indeed be dying if he sent for Madame de Fonblanque.

So terrible and so piteous is death that
every one of them, who a moment before had
been discussing the dying man with severity,
felt that he or she would do much to save him.
Even Madame de Fonblanque turned pale.

"Of course, I will go," she said, "perhaps
he wants my forgiveness — or to repair the
injury he has done me."

She went hastily up-stairs, Letty with her,
to put on her wraps to go to the house from
which only a few hours before she had been
ignominiously shown. The Colonel would
by no means allow her to go alone, and when
she came down, she found him with his great-
coat on, and a large pair of "gambadoes"
strapped around his legs to protect his
trousers, in case he should have to get out on
the road in the snow and slush. In a few
moments, they were on their way in the bit-

ter night toward Shrewsbury, the Colonel's
saddle horse following the carriage.

Letty and Farebrother and Miss Jemima,
sitting in the library, determined to wait until
midnight, certainly, for some news of the
dying man or the Colonel's return.   In spite
of the happiness of the lovers, there was a
cloud upon Farebrother and Letty.   Not a
word was said about Mr. Romaine's will.   All
of them were more or less skeptical about it,
but still his death was deeply impressive to
them.   At one o'clock, they were still sitting
there, talking gravely, when they heard the
returning carriage, and presently the Colonel
stalked solemnly in, and Madame de Fonblanque in much agitation with him.

XII

T was only four miles to Shrewsbury, and Dodson did not spare
the horses, but it took them an
hour to make it, and it was ten o'clock before
they drew up to the door. Madame de Fonblanque had remained perfectly silent during
the drive. But the Colonel, remembering that
he must, of necessity, soon go the perilous
way that Mr. Romaine was now traversing,
was all remorse. He reproached himself for
his estrangement from Mr. Romaine, and remembered only their boyhood together, when
they had been really fond of one another.

As the carriage crunched along the drive
across the lawn, the house door opened, and
Mrs. Chessingham appeared. The Colonel
assisted Madame de Fonblanque up the steps,
and in the full glare of the light Mrs. Chessingham saw the woman that had made such a
commotion the night before. She was struck

by the dignity of Madame de Fonblanque's bearing, and could imagine how even so fastidious a person as Mr. Romaine might be fascinated by her.

"He has been asking for you for the last half hour," she said, helping Madame de Fonblanque off with her wraps, and escorting her to the door of Mr. Romaine's library.

Mr. Chessingham came out with a troubled face, and, closing the door behind him, was presented to Madame de Fonblanque.

"Do you think he is dying?" she asked.

"Undoubtedly. And he knows it himself, and is perfectly prepared, but when I ventured to hint as much to him, he told me he thought Carlsbad was the place for him, and he was going there next summer."

A faint smile appeared upon the faces of all three. Majestic death was at hand, but Mr. Romaine had to have his quip with the Destroyer before going upon the great journey.

"And I frankly admit," said Chessingham, worried almost beyond bearing, "that Mr. Romaine has never yet told me what ailed him, and I do not know any more than you do what he is dying of. I suspect, of course — but it may be one of a half dozen things,

any one of which would be equally fatal. He
will not let me know his pulse, temperature, or
anything, and his perversity about his symptoms is simply phenomenal. He will not even
be undressed and go to bed. If you will
believe me, he had his evening clothes put on
him, and there he sits, dying."

Madame de Fonblanque, without another
word, advanced and opened the door for herself, shutting it carefully after her.

There, indeed, sat Mr. Romaine in his easy
chair, with his feet in exquisite dancing pumps.
stretched out to the fire. His face was ghastly
white — but as it was always white, it did not
make a great deal of difference. His eyes,
though, were quite unchanged — in fact, they
seemed to glow with an added fire and bril-
liance. Still, he was plainly dying.

"I came as soon as you sent for me," said
Madame de Fonblanque, gently. "I want to
say now, that if you think I bear you any
anger for anything you have said or done to
me, you are mistaken. I forget it all as I
look at you."

"Did you think I sent for you to ask your
forgiveness?" asked Mr. Romaine, faintly, but
fluently.

"I can think of no other reason."

"Then you must be a very unimaginative person. I sent for you to punish you as you deserve. It won't make life any pleasanter for you to know that you helped me out of it. I have had, for some years, as you know, an affection which the doctors told me any agitation or distress might make fatal. I might have lived for years — but your presence here last night was my death blow. I don't care a rush about living,— in fact, I would rather die than suffer as I do now,— but I would have lived possibly ten years longer, but for you."

"Pray do not say that," cried Madame de Fonblanque, turning pale. "Think what a painful thought to follow one through life."

"That 's why I tell you."

"Pray, pray withdraw it," cried Madame de Fonblanque, in tears. "I implore you."

"You would not withdraw your demand for one hundred thousand francs. If you had — if you had shown me the slightest mercy, there is a way by which I might have rewarded you. I could have borrowed a good deal of money upon some few pictures I have in Europe. But forced under the hammer, they

will not bring, with this Virginia land, more
than enough to pay my debts and a few
legacies." He stopped a moment, out of
breath, and the silence was only broken by
Madame de Fonblanque's faint sobs.

" Nobody has ever yet relied upon my generosity without experiencing it. But everybody that has ever fought me, I have made to
rue it," he continued.

Madame de Fonblanque sank kneeling by
his chair, and wept nervously.

" Will you — forgive me? You must."

" Rubbish !"

" And are you not afraid to go into that
other world with a fellow creature crying after
you from this for forgiveness ? "

" Not a bit. I never knew what fear was.
Pain, instead of making me fear death, has
rendered me totally indifferent to it. I am
astonished at myself now, that I feel so little
apprehension."

Madame de Fonblanque got up from her
knees. Living or dying, he was unlike other
men.

"Now," said he, " I want you to make me a
promise. Dying people's requests are sacred,

you know. Perhaps if you oblige me in this instance, I may oblige you later on. Will you promise?"

"Yes," answered Madame de Fonblanque, unable to say no.

"I desire that you remain alone with me until I am dead. It is coming now. I feel it."

Madame de Fonblanque remained silent with horror. A frightful paroxysm of pain came on, and after standing the sight of him writhing for a few moments, she fled shrieking from the room.

An instant later she returned with Chessingham. Mr. Romaine had then recovered from his spasm of pain, and greeted her sarcastically.

"You have broken your promise," he said.

Chessingham came up to him anxiously. He proposed a dozen alleviations of the pain, but Mr. Romaine would not agree to any.

"Look here, Chessingham," he said, "the game is up. I am dying, and I might as well own it. I have n't taken a dose of your medicine since I employed you as my doctor. I consulted Chambers on the sly, and studied up my case myself — and I have a whole pharmacopœia that you never saw or heard of. It was

rather shabby of me, I acknowledge; but I
liked you and thought you were a capital
fellow, and I wanted your company, and the
only way I could get you was to make you my
doctor."

Chessingham said nothing. He could not
reproach a dying man, but his stern face spoke
volumes.

"And you are one of the most honest fellows
in the world. Don't think I disbelieve in honesty. I believe in a great many good things.
I even believe in a Great First Cause. I have
only followed the natural law: those that have
been good to me, I have been good to —
and those that have n't been good to me, I
have taken the liberty of paying off in this
world, for fear that by some hocus-pocus they
might sneak out of punishment in the next."

"I want to say one thing to you," said Chessingham. "I never have considered you a
bad man. But your virtues are not common
virtues, and your faults are not common faults."

"Thank you, my dear fellow. It is true, I
never could strike the great vein of common-
place in anything."

Then there was a pause. Mr. Romaine,
though evidently suffering, yet continued to

talk until Madame de Fonblanque whispered
to Chessingham:

"I believe he actually enjoys the situation!"

She herself longed to leave, yet hesitated.
She thought if she stayed that perhaps at
the end Mr. Romaine might grant her some
words of forgiveness. She was a superstitious
woman, and Mr. Romaine knew it. So, with
a white face, she seated herself a little way
off, at the side of the fireplace. Bridge came
in and out of the room noiselessly, his feet
sinking in the thick Turkish carpet. The
room was strangely quiet, but the very intensity
of the silence gave Mr. Romaine's voice and
quivering breath and faint sounds of pain a
fearful distinctness. And even in his extremity, the "situation," as Madame de Fonblanque
called it, was not without its diversion to him.

"Corbin came with you, of course," Mr. Romaine said to Madame de Fonblanque after a
while. He had at last consented to take a little brandy, although steadily refusing any of
Chessingham's medicine, and seemed to be re-
vived by it. Then he said to Chessingham:

"Pray, after I am dead, give my regards to
Corbin, but don't let him examine my coffin
plate. I desire my age put down as fifty-eight,
and I won't have one of Corbin's long-winded

arguments to prove that I am sixty-nine. Still,
Corbin is a good fellow. But if there were
many like him, the rascals would soon have a
handsome majority everywhere. And I also
wish my regards given to Mrs. Chessingham
and Miss Maywood, and my apologies for dis-
appointing them regarding the season in London. And also to Letty Corbin," and Mr. Romaine paused, and his face softened.

"Say to Jemima Corbin, if I ever caused
her pain I now ask her forgiveness for it."

This surprised both Chessingham and Madame de Fonblanque much, who knew of no
reason why Mr. Romaine should send such a
message to good Miss Jemima.

It was now about eleven o'clock. Mr. Romaine was evidently going fast, but he still
managed to resist being laid on the sofa.

"You will last longer," said Chessingham.

"I don't care to last any longer than I can
help," snapped Mr. Romaine, in what Farebrother had called his Romainesque manner.

"My will is in that drawer," he said, with
some difficulty. "It will cause a good deal of
surprise," and his teeth showed in a ghastly
smile between his blue lips, "and also a letter
for Madame de Fonblanque."

At the last Mr. Romaine fell into a stupor.

Presently he opened his eyes, and looking Chessingham full in the face, said in a pleasant voice, "Good-night."

"Good-night," responded Chessingham; and before the words were out of his mouth Mr. Romaine had ceased to breathe.

Madame de Fonblanque rushed to the door, as she had been on the point of doing every moment she had been in the room. Bridge followed her, and caught her out in the hall.

"Madam," he said, "I wants to say as I heard what Mr. Romaine said to you about your givin' 'im 'is death blow. Mr. Romaine has been a-dyin' for a month — and it s'prised me he lasted so long. I say this because it 's my dooty."

"Thank you," cried Madame de Fonblanque.

Mrs. Chessingham, Colonel Corbin, and Ethel Maywood were all gathered in the hall when Chessingham came out with a solemn face. Ethel was white and trembling, and felt a strange grief at knowing that Mr. Romaine was no more. There were no tears shed. All of them had at some time received kindnesses from Mr. Romaine, but also all of them had experienced the iron hand under the velvet glove. Madame de Fonblanque could not get away from the house fast enough, and so the same carriage that had brought them there landed them at Corbin Hall about one o'clock.

Farebrother, Letty, and Miss Jemima were still up. The fire had been kept going, although the lamp had long since given out. Colonel Corbin's face told the story. A pause fell, as in the hall at Shrewsbury, and in the shadows Miss Jemima wiped two tears from her withered face. They were the only tears shed for Mr. Romaine.

Madame de Fonblanque's nerve quite forsook her. She felt that she must get away from that place, so associated with tragic things, or die. It had suddenly moderated, and a warm rain had set in by midnight that was certain to break up the ice in the river. She begged and implored the Colonel to take her to the landing on the chance of the boat passing. Colonel Corbin could not say no to her pleading — and so, in the dimness of early dawn, she disappeared like a shadow that had come from another world and had gone back to it.

XIII

AS soon as the funeral was over came the reading of the will. On the outside was the request, written in Mr. Romaine's own hand, that it be read by Chessingham, whom he appointed his executor in case he died in America — for in his own country there was scarcely a person with whom Mr. Romaine was upon terms of any close association. The request was also made that Colonel Corbin and Miss Letty Corbin be present when the will was read, and any one else that Chessingham desired.

On the day following the one when Mr. Romaine had been laid in the old burying-ground beside his fathers, Chessingham wrote a note to Colonel and Miss Corbin, inviting their presence upon a certain day at Shrewsbury, and although Mr. Romaine had not mentioned any of his numerous tribes of nephews and nieces, Chessingham scrupulously invited them all. Farebrother, who found it very pleasant lingering at Corbin Hall as Letty's lover, of course did not accompany the Corbins to Shrewsbury. Like Letty, he would have been pleased to have money "honestly come by," so to speak; but the idea of having it under the circumstances from Mr. Romaine appeared to him as undesirable as it did to her.

"And I tell you now," said Letty, firmly, to Farebrother, as he stood on the old porch in the wintry sunshine waiting for Dad Davy (who superseded Tom Battercake on important occasions like this) with the ramshackly carriage; "I tell you now, I don't want that money, and I shall at once consult a lawyer to see if it can't be turned over to the people it rightfully belongs to. It would make me wretched to know of those poor people — I know how poor they are and out at elbows — actually in want, while I should have what was their grandfather's and their uncle's."

"All right," answered Farebrother, "and I would prefer that you should have the whole thing settled before we are married, so you can act as a perfectly free agent. As for me, if I can have you," etc., etc., etc. — which may be interpreted in the language of lovers.

Arrived at Shrewsbury, it was seen that every relative of Mr. Romaine had accepted Chessingham's invitation and was on hand. Letty had to run the gantlet of their hostile eyes as she entered the library, for the great affair had already leaked out. The room looked strangely suggestive of Mr. Romaine. Letty could scarcely persuade herself that at any moment his slight figure and sparkling black eyes would not appear.

Mrs. Chessingham and Ethel were in the room by special request of Colonel Corbin, who thought it a mark of respect. When they were all assembled, Chessingham, who had worn a very peculiar look, began to speak in the midst of a solemn silence.

" As you are perhaps aware, our late friend, Mr. Romaine, desired me to act as his executor in case he died in this country — a contingency which he seemed to think likely when he came here, less than a year ago. In pursuance of my duties, I have examined his papers, which are very few, and find everything concerning him to have been in perfect order for many years past, so that if he had died at any moment there would have been no difficulty in settling his affairs. But I soon discov-

ered a very important fact — which is," — here
he spoke with deliberate emphasis, — " that instead of Mr. Romaine possessing a large fortune, as the world has always supposed, he had
invested everything he had in — annuities —
which gave him a very large income — but he
left but little behind him."

A kind of groan went round among the poor
relations. Letty, who understood quickly what
was meant, felt dazed; she did not know
whether she was glad or sorry.

Chessingham exhibited some papers, showing, in Mr. Romaine's writing, the amounts of
various annuities, which aggregated a magnificent income. Then came a list of his actual
property, which consisted chiefly of the Shrewsbury place and the Virginia lands, but which
were heavily mortgaged. His personal property was remarkably small; Mr. Romaine had
always boasted his freedom from impedimenta.
And then began the reading of the will. It was
the same brief document that Chessingham
and Miss Maywood had witnessed. Some of
the nieces and nephews got a few thousand
dollars. Chessingham got his *douceur*, Miss
Maywood got the diamonds in a codicil witnessed by Bridge and Dodson, and Letty was

left "residuary legatee" by a person who had nothing to give. When she walked out of the Shrewsbury house she was not any richer than when she went in it. But before that Colonel Corbin had risen and in a very dignified and forcible manner read the correspondence that had passed between Mr. Romaine and himself and Letty, which showed conclusively that they were in no way parties to Mr. Romaine's scheme, but rather victims of it. Then Chessingham, replying to a formal question of the Colonel's, admitted that there would be in all probability not enough property to pay the legacies in full, and the Colonel and Letty retired, having no further interest in Mr. Romaine's affairs.

When they got home Farebrother ran down the steps to meet them.

"I sha'n't get a penny, and I'm glad of it," cried out Letty, from the carriage, before Farebrother could open the door.

"Wait until you have struggled along in New York on four or five thousand a year before you say that," answered Farebrother in a gay whisper which quite escaped the Colonel, who knew, however, how the land lay.

Farebrother stayed two weeks altogether at Corbin Hall on that visit; and before he left Sir Archibald Corbin arrived.

The status of affairs looked decidedly unpleasant to Sir Archy. After he had been there a day or two, he went for a walk with Letty in the woods — the very path they had taken that autumn evening two months before — and Sir Archy presently demanded to know if she was engaged to Farebrother.

"What a very singular inquiry," replied Letty, haughtily. "Surely you can't expect me to answer it."

"I would scarcely expect you to hesitate about denying it if it were not true — and if it were true, and you kept it a secret, it would be a very grave reflection on you, which I should be loath to entertain," responded Sir Archy, with equal haughtiness.

"A reflection on me to be engaged to Mr. Farebrother," cried Letty, whirling around on him.

"I meant, of course, secretly," answered Sir Archy, stiffly.

"Do you mean to say that I would be guilty of the shocking indelicacy of proclaiming my engagement to the world — if I *were* engaged to Mr. Farebrother — as if I had just landed a big fish?"

"Our ideas of delicacy differ widely. There seems to me an indelicacy in a secret engagement."

Sir Archy was very angry — but Letty was simply boiling with rage. Both were right from their respective points of view, but neither had the slightest understanding of the other.

After that there was no further staying at Corbin Hall for Sir Archy. He escorted Letty to the door, and then tramped off to Shrewsbury and sent for his luggage.

The Chessinghams remained at the Romaine place for the present, awaiting their speedy return to England.

Letty went into the house, nearly crying with rage. Farebrother, who was to leave the next day, met her and received the account, red hot, of Sir Archy's rude remarks, with shouts of laughter which very much offended Letty.

"I don't see anything to laugh at," she said, with pretty sullenness.

"I see everything to laugh at," answered Farebrother, going off again. He did not further explain the joke to Letty, who never quite fully comprehended it.

Sir Archy, stalking along toward Shrewsbury, smarting under his disappointment —
for he really admired Letty, and had fully
meant to offer her the chance of becoming
Lady Corbin — yet felt a sort of secret relief.
Letty was the soul of bright purity, but as Sir
Archy philosophically argued, no matter how
right people's characters may be, if their ideas
are radically wrong, it sooner or later affects
their characters.

" And that fatal want of prudence," reasoned
this English-minded gentleman, "this reck-
lessness concerning her relations with men, is
a most grave consideration.   She appears totally unable to take a serious view of anything
in the relations of young men and women.
Life seems to be to her one long flirtation.
And she may, of course, be expected to keep
this up after she is married.   On the whole,
although a fascinating creature, I should call
it a dangerous experiment to marry her."

So thought Sir Archy concerning Letty,
who was of a type that is apt to develop into
the most cloying domesticity.

Then his thoughts wandered to Ethel Maywood.   He was too sincere and too earnest a
man to cast his heart immediately at Ethel's

feet — but something in his glance that very
night made Ethel and the Chessinghams think
that perhaps, in the end, Miss Maywood's
name might be Lady Corbin.

The first step toward this followed some
days after.   Sir Archy had continued to stay
at Shrewsbury, much to Colonel Corbin's chagrin.   He had divined that there had been a
falling out of some sort between Letty and
Sir Archy — but he was quite unable to get
at the particulars.   Each professed a willingness to make up, and upon Sir Archy's paying
a formal visit at Corbin Hall, Letty came
down to see him and they were stiffly polite.
But their misunderstanding seemed, as it was,
deep rooted.   Letty felt a profound displeasure
with a man who could, even by implication,
accuse her of indelicacy — and Sir Archy had
grave doubts upon the score of Letty's knowledge of good form, to put it mildly.

It was on this subject that he grew confidential with Ethel, and made the longest
speech of his life.

"You see," he said, "at first I found those
American young ladies who imitate English
girls rather a bore, as most of us do.   When
we go in for an English girl, we like the real

thing — sweet, genuine, and wholesome. But
at least the ideas of these pseudo-English
girls are correct. They are not flirts "—
Sir Archy classed flirts as the feminine
form of barnburners and horse thieves — "and
there 's nothing clandestine in their way of
arranging marriages. They are quite candid
and correct in that matter. They receive the
attentions of men properly, and when an engagement is made, it is duly and promptly
announced. But my cousin, Miss Corbin, has
the most extraordinary notions on the subject
of the proprieties. She goes according to the
rule of contrary. She thinks it no harm to
make eyes at every man she sees, without
caring a button about any one of them — and
an engagement is a thing to be concealed as
if it were something to be ashamed of. I
confess it puzzles me."

" And it puzzles me, too," replied Ethel.
" Of course I know how sincerely high minded
Miss Corbin is, but, like you, I can't reconcile
myself to her peculiar notions. Do you remember the evening we went to the theater
in New York and she wore that astonishing
white gown ? "

"Yes — and uncommonly pretty she looked.

But it was bad form — decidedly bad form —
and she never seemed to suspect it. My
cousin is charming, but unusual and unac-
countable."

Which Miss Maywood felt a profound satisfaction in hearing.

It was a month or two before the Chessinghams sailed. Although Mr. Romaine's affairs
were so well arranged, the sale of the landed
property could not take place at once, and
Chessingham concluded to return to England,
and come back in a year's time to settle up
the small estate. The more he looked into it,
the more convinced he was that Mr. Romaine's
residuary legatee would get nothing, and
that Mr. Romaine knew it; and his object
was merely that contrary impulse and the
natural perversity and desire to disconcert
people which always gave him acute delight.

Colonel Corbin and Letty were sincerely
sorry to part from the Chessinghams, but
Letty bore the coming privation of Miss
Maywood's society with the utmost fortitude.
When they went over to say good-by on an
early spring afternoon, Letty noticed a peculiarly joyous look on Ethel's fair face. In a
little while she proposed a walk in the old-

fashioned garden. The two girls strolled together down the box-edged walk, and passed
under the quaint old arbors, heavy with the
yellow jessamine, just beginning then to show
the faintly budding leaves. There was something melancholy in the scene. The place
had been deserted for so long — and it was
now for sale, with the prospect of soon passing
into other hands. The graveyard, with its
high brick wall, was just below the garden,
and, although she could not see it, Letty was
conscious of a new white tombstone there with
Mr. Romaine's name and "aged 58" engraved
upon it — which last had caused Colonel
Corbin much dissatisfaction. But Chessingham preferred to carry out what he knew to
be Mr. Romaine's wishes in the matter, and
believed that his ghost would have walked
had his real age been proclaimed upon his
monument.

As soon as the two girls were well in the
garden, Ethel began, with a glowing face:

"I have had great happiness lately."

"Have you?" asked Letty, sympathetically.
"What is it?"

"I am engaged to Sir Archibald Corbin,"
said Ethel, looking into Letty's face with a

bright smile.   Letty was so shocked by Miss Maywood's candor that she stood quite still, and said "Oh!" in a grieved voice, which Miss Maywood took to mean regret at having lost the prize.

"As everybody knows you are engaged to Mr. Farebrother," continued Ethel, still smiling, and twisting off a twig of syringa that was at hand, "you can't grudge me my good fortune."

Grudge her her good fortune! And "everybody" knowing she was engaged to Farebrother, when she had not breathed a word of it outside her own family, albeit she had half her trousseau finished! Letty was so scandalized by Miss Maywood's brazen assurance, as she regarded it, that she could only say, coldly:

"I do not understand how 'everybody' can know that I am engaged to Mr. Farebrother. Certainly I have never mentioned it, and I am sure that he has n't."

"That 's only your odd Southern way," answered Ethel, disapprovingly.

Curiosity got the better of Letty's disgust, and she asked, "How long have you and my cousin been engaged?"

"Only to-day," calmly replied Ethel. "Reg-

gie brought the letter from the postoffice this
morning, and I answered it at once.   I also
wrote to England, in order to catch the next
steamer.   Sir Archy is in New York, and won't
get my letter for two days perhaps.   Reggie
and Gladys and I have talked over the engagement a little this afternoon.   I shall be
married very quietly in the country — we
have an uncle who is a clergyman, and he
has a nice parish, and will be glad to have me
married from the rectory — and Reggie and
Gladys very sensibly don't expect me to marry
a baronet from their London lodgings.   Sir
Archy was very explicit in his letter about our
future plans.   He is willing to spend a month
in London this season, but he has been away
so much he feels it necessary to be at Fox
Court in June — and he has taken a place in
Scotland from the 12th of August."

"But suppose you did n't care to go to
Scotland from the 12th of August?   And suppose you wanted to spend more than a month
in London?" asked Letty, much scandalized by
these cut and dried proceedings.

"Of course I should not make the slightest
objection to any of Sir Archy's plans," replied
Ethel, wonderingly.

"And he must have assumed a good deal," suddenly cried Letty, bursting out laughing.

" He only assumed that I would act as any other sensible girl would," replied Ethel, calmly. "Sir Archy is a baronet of good family, suitable age, and excellent estate. What more could a girl — and a girl in my position —want?"

"Nothing in the world, I fancy," answered Letty, laughing still more ; and when the two girls had their last interview they misunderstood and disesteemed each other more than at their first.

Driving home through the odorous dusk, in the chaise by the Colonel's side, Letty pondered over the remarkable ways of some people. The idea of a man dictating his plans to a woman before he married her — or after, for that matter. Farebrother had asked her what she would like, and their plans were made solely and entirely by Letty. "But I think," she reflected, as she laid her pretty head back in the chaise, "that I would do whatever he asked me to do — because, after all, he is twice the man that my cousin Archy is, and deserves to be loved twice as much —" and " he " meant Farebrother, who was, at that very moment, working hard for Letty in his office on a noisy New York thoroughfare. And when his work was done, he turned for refreshment to a photograph of her which he kept in that breast pocket reserved for such articles, and gazed fondly at her face in its starlike purity — and then smiled. He never looked at Letty or thought of her that, along with the most tender respect, he did not feel like smiling ; and Letty never could and never did understand why it was that Farebrother found her such an amusing study.

www.ingramcontent.com/pod-product-compliance
Lightning Source LLC
Chambersburg PA
CBHW030618030726
47497CB00006B/1549